Hannah wasn't surprised when Colin turned in early for the night.

With his brother sleeping in the room next to him, there had been no chance he'd invite Hannah into his bed. Still, logic didn't stop her from lying awake long past midnight on the slim hope that he might knock against her bedroom door. His scent lingered on her sheets and the memories of what they'd done in this very bed earlier in the day tormented her.

It would be easy to blame Justin for his inconvenient timing, but with or without his showing up, the end result was going to be the same. She would lose Colin. He'd never made any secret that he wasn't the kind of guy to stick around in one place. He'd always planned to leave for his brother's wedding and that job afterward on a cattle drive. Although she'd enjoyed hearing Justin's anecdotes about wedding plans, each one reminded her that the big day was rapidly approaching.

Her time with Colin was almost at an end.

She blinked rapidly, trying to catch her tears on her lashes. It didn't count as crying over the cowboy if the tears didn't actually make it to her cheeks.

Find a bright side, her inner voice urged. Like... the ranch was in far better shape than it had been before Colin had come.

But what about me? What shape would her heart be in once he'd gone?.

Dear Reader,

Isn't it frustrating—even heartbreaking—when bad things happen to good people? Over the years, I've witnessed a few friends stagger through hard times, seemingly plagued by one tragedy after another. But they've inspired me with their resilience and spirit, weathering numerous difficulties and rediscovering joy.

Colin Cade is a man who has experienced a great deal of difficulty and loss—his parents' deaths when he was young and, more recently, the deaths of his wife and child in a car accident. For months afterward, all that held him together was the support of his two siblings. But his sister is now busy with her newborn daughter, and his brother is engaged and neck-deep in wedding plans. They're moving forward with their lives, and Colin decides to move on, too. He does odd jobs on ranches, never staying in one place for long, never getting attached.

Until he meets young widow Hannah Shaw and her four-year-old son. Working alongside Hannah at the Silver Linings Ranch changes Colin's perspective, reminding him that loss doesn't have to define a person. But even as he heals, he questions whether he's brave enough to love again.

Colin and Hannah were one of my favorite couples to write, and I hope that you find their story as poignant and uplifting as I do. Please drop by on Facebook (AuthorTanyaMichaels) or Twitter (@TanyaMichaels) and let me know!

Best wishes,

Tanya

HER COWBOY HERO

—

Tanya Michaels

Happy reading!

Tanya Michaels

RWA14

HARLEQUIN® AMERICAN ROMANCE®

ISBN-13: 978-0-373-75522-6

HER COWBOY HERO

HARLEQUIN®
™ www.Harlequin.com

Printed in U.S.A.

ABOUT THE AUTHOR

New York Times bestselling author and three-time RITA® Award nominee Tanya Michaels writes about what she knows—community, family and lasting love! Her books, praised for their poignancy and humor, have received honors such as a Booksellers' Best Bet Award, a Maggie Award of Excellence and multiple readers' choice awards. She was also a 2010 *RT Book Reviews* nominee for Career Achievement in Category Romance. Tanya is an active member of Romance Writers of America and a frequent public speaker, presenting workshops to educate and encourage aspiring writers. She lives outside Atlanta with her very supportive husband, two highly imaginative children and a household of quirky pets, including a cat who thinks she's a dog and a bichon frise who thinks she's the center of the universe.

Books by Tanya Michaels

This is dedicated to everyone who emailed and posted online after reading the first Colorado Cades book to say they couldn't wait for Colin's story!

Chapter One

For Colin Cade, one of the chief selling points of his motorcycle had been solitude. He preferred being alone, making it a conscious choice rather than a tragic circumstance, but that meant a lot of time in his own head. Unfortunately, not even the Harley could outrun his thoughts. Or his anger.

How the hell had he—a man who'd lived like a monk for the better part of two years—been fired for "sexual misconduct"?

Raising younger siblings had taught him patience the hard way, but right now his temper was providing uncharacteristic daydreams of shaking Delia McCoy's shoulders until her professionally whitened teeth rattled. She'd had no business showing up naked in his bed. The more he thought about it, the more convinced he was that his former employer's wife didn't even want an affair. There had been plenty of other men working the ranch who would have taken advantage of her adulterous offer. So why target the guy who'd never once returned her flirtatious smiles? Was it possible she only wanted to shock Sean McCoy into paying more attention to her? Ranches took a lot of work, and Delia had complained to anyone who would listen that her husband neglected her.

Maybe she had cause to be bitter, but that sure didn't give her the right to screw up Colin's life.

He was supposed to have stayed on at the McCoy place for another month. The McCoys were crossbreeding Angus and Hereford cows, and Colin, the former owner of a large-animal vet practice, had been hired to help deliver calves and see them off to a healthy start. His job would have included routine disease prevention and facilitating adoption for the expected twin sets and any heifers that lost their babies. His next contract—helping move two herds to the high country for summer grazing—was all lined up, but the cattle drive was nearly six weeks away, after his brother's wedding.

What was he supposed to do in the meantime?

An old trail guide acquaintance had given him a possible lead, but he had sounded skeptical about it. "There's a lady in the northwest, not far from where I hired on, who's been looking for help. The Widow Shaw. None of the qualified ranch hands will waste time working for her, because her place is going belly-up any day now. Everyone knows it 'cept her. Frail little thing is clearly addled. Bakes the best rum cake I've ever had in my life, though."

Despite his friend's warning, Colin thought the job sounded promising enough to head for Bingham Pass and call on the Widow Shaw.

After his last two jobs—which had included the naked Mrs. McCoy and, prior to that, a moony-eyed teenage daughter of a foreman in Routt County—an elderly, absentminded woman who liked to bake sounded perfect. Colin wouldn't stay long, but while he was there, he'd do what he could to get her back on her feet. And if that proved impossible…well, life sucked sometimes.

Who knew that better than him?

INHALING DEEPLY, HANNAH SHAW took stock of her situation. The early evening sky was starting to darken sooner than it should, and she had a flat tire on a stretch of road where cell service was nonexistent. How was it possible that astronauts could tweet from space, but there were still places in modern Colorado where a woman couldn't get bars on her phone?

Bright side, Hannah. Find the bright side. After four years, her mantra was automatic. She tried every day to keep the vow she'd made in that hospital bed, to live with courageous optimism. Of course, that vow was currently being challenged by unyielding loan officers and the countless maintenance issues she'd inherited along with the Shaw family ranch. But she hadn't survived this long by whining or embracing negativity.

The silver lining here was that Evan was spending the night at her friend Annette's house instead of watching with worried eyes from his booster seat. Also, Hannah had successfully changed a flat tire once before, so there was no reason to think she couldn't do it again. If the problem had been, say, her carburetor, she'd really be screwed.

"I got this," she muttered, flipping on her hazard lights. She wished she'd been able to move the truck farther off the road, but there wasn't exactly a reliable shoulder on these winding curves. She shrugged out of the lightweight blazer she'd borrowed from Annette. Beneath it, Hannah wore a white blouse that strained at the buttons down her chest, a premotherhood relic from the back of her closet. It was one of the few items in her wardrobe professional enough for a bank meeting, and the neatly buttoned jacket had camouflaged the imperfect fit.

As she twisted her long black hair up in an elastic band, she tried not to dwell on the banker's condescending expression. She'd once again been told that maybe *after* she made significant improvements on the ranch, demonstrating that it was a solid investment, she could reapply. How was she supposed to make "significant" improvements without funds? She'd planned to rename the spread the Silver Linings Ranch, but it might be more accurate to call it The Catch-22. She'd received money after Michael's death, of course, but a good chunk of that was in savings for Evan. Despite her careful planning—and the money she'd set aside to hire competent help—she had underestimated how much work the ranch would need before she could realize her plans.

One thing at a time. Fix the tire now, save the ranch tomorrow.

She climbed down from the cab and went to the back of the truck, where the tools and spare tire were kept under a cover that could be worth more than the vehicle. *Note to self: maybe you should start keeping spare work clothes in the bed of the truck.* While she wouldn't necessarily mourn the ruination of the tight blouse, getting on the ground to change the tire was going to be murder on her pretty navy skirt.

A rumble of thunder echoed off the surrounding mountains, confirming Hannah's suspicions about the prematurely dark sky. Rain hadn't been in the forecast until tomorrow, but spring storms could move fast. Which meant she had better move fast, too.

Hurrying, she found a couple of good-size rocks on the side of the road to place in front of the tires. She was reluctant to completely trust the pickup's emergency brake. The air seemed to crackle with expectancy, and wind whipped around her, chilling her skin. She'd only ever changed the tire on a car, and there had been a notch where the jack belonged. The truck did not have one. She was feeling around, trying to determine the correct place for the jack so she didn't crack anything on the undercarriage, when the sky opened. Fat drops pelted her with enough force to sting.

But on the bright side, after a couple of years of drought, ranchers like her really needed the rain.

THE SHOWER HAD moved in fast, catching Colin by surprise. He'd anticipated getting into town before the rain started. He was scanning the side of the road for possible shelter when he rounded the curve and saw a stopped truck.

A woman knelt by a tire in the path of traffic. Not that there were any cars in sight, but lives could be taken in an instant. Stifling unwelcome memories—the call from the hospital, the twisted wreckage—he steered his motorcycle off the road and lifted his helmet.

"Need a hand?" he called over the rain.

The woman stood and he realized that, while she didn't even reach his shoulder, she wasn't tiny everywhere. She looked like the generously endowed winner of a wet T-shirt contest. A blouse that had probably once been white but was now translucent was plastered to an equally see-through lace bra. He abruptly glanced away but not before catching a glimpse of dark, puckered nipples.

In one motion, he ripped off his leather jacket and shoved it toward her. "Here."

"Thanks." Cheeks flushed with color, she accepted the coat, her hazel eyes not quite meeting his.

Watching her put on his clothing felt uncomfortably intimate, and he found himself annoyed with her for being here, in his path. "Don't you have some kind of road service you could call?"

"Even if I did, there's no reception here. But I'm not incapable of—"

"Wait in the cab," he ordered. "No sense in both of us getting drenched."

Her posture went rigid, and she drew herself up to her full—what, five feet? But she didn't argue. "Far be it from me to look a gift Samaritan in the mouth." Once inside, she rolled down the window. Literally. The truck had one of the manual window cranks that had been replaced with electric buttons in most modern vehicles. She seemed to be supervising his work.

"This truck is ancient," he said. "God knows why you're driving it when the kinder thing would be to shoot it and put it out of its misery."

"It's not *that* bad," she retorted. Was that indignation or worry in her tone? "It just needs a little TLC."

He grunted, focusing on getting the tire changed. Stomping on the wrench to loosen the lug nut felt good. He was in the mood to kick something's ass. By the time he had the spare in place, the rain had shifted to a heavy drizzle. Ominous black clouds rolled closer. The storm might be taking a coffee break, but it hadn't quit.

"That spare's not going to get you far," he warned. "It's in lousy shape. Kind of like the rest of this heap."

His disdain encompassed the replacement door that was a different color from the body of the truck and a side mirror that looked loose.

She met his contempt with a half smile. "On the bright side, getting the flat gave me a chance to rest the engine and let the radiator cool down. Don't worry, my ranch is only a few miles away. In fact, you should come with me. Wait out the storm. Judging from those clouds, we're in for a lot worse."

Although he recognized the logic in her words, the invitation irked him. "Lady, I could be a serial killer. You don't invite strangers home with you."

"Not normally, no." Her hazel eyes darkened, her expression somber. "If it helps, I was taught self-defense by a marine and I'm a lot tougher than I look."

A sizzle of lightning struck close enough to make both of them start.

"You shouldn't be riding that motorcycle in this," she scolded. For a split second, she reminded him of his sister, Arden. Not all women were so at ease bossing around grown men who towered over them. He wondered if Hazel Eyes had brothers. If they worked on that ranch she'd mentioned, it could explain why she wasn't worried about bringing a total stranger home with her.

"Come on," she prompted, impatience creeping into her tone as more lightning flashed. "I have enough problems without picking up my morning paper and seeing that you got fried to the asphalt."

He didn't realize he was going to agree until the words left his mouth. "Lead the way." He hadn't been there the day a car accident had shattered his world, hadn't been able to do a damn thing to help. He found he couldn't abandon this woman until she and her rattling joke of a truck were out of the rain.

Mounting his bike, he shook his head at the unexpected turn of events. Hazel was not the first woman who'd invited him back to her place. But it was the first time in two years that he'd accepted.

COLIN WAS TOO occupied with the diminishing visibility and handling his bike on the dirt road to study his surroundings. He had a general impression of going through a gated entrance; farther ahead were much larger structures, likely the main house and a barn or stable. But the truck stopped at a narrow, one-story building.

The woman parked in the mud, gesturing out her window that he should go around and park beneath the covered carport, where the motorcycle would be out of the worst of the elements. She joined him under the carport a moment later, her hand tucked inside the purse she wore over her shoulder. He wondered if she had pepper spray or a Taser in there. She'd sounded serious when she mentioned the self-defense lessons.

"This is the old bunkhouse," she said. "I'm about to start refurbing it as a guest cabin, but at the moment it's mostly empty."

He supposed that any brothers or a husband lived in the main house with her. Although what caring husband would let his wife drive a disaster on wheels like that truck?

She tossed him a key ring and nodded toward the door. "You can get a hot shower, dry off. There's a microwave and a few cans of soup in the cabinet. Before you tell me I'm naive and that you might be a master burglar, let me assure you there's nothing to steal. I doubt you could get thirty bucks on Craigslist for the twin bed and microwave combined."

He unlocked the door, noting how she kept a casual but unmistakable distance. Once he'd flipped the light switch, he saw that she was right about the lack of luxuries. The "carpet" was the kind of multipurpose indoor/outdoor covering used more in screened patios than homes. There was enough space for three or four beds, but only one was pushed against the wall. At one end of the long, rectangular interior was a minifridge and microwave, at the other a bathroom. Aside from a couple of truly ugly paintings of cows, the place was barren.

He stopped in the center of the room, raising an eyebrow. "The minifridge brings up my Craigslist asking price to thirty-five."

She gave a sharp laugh, abruptly stifled. "Sorry the accommodations aren't classier. The ranch is…in a rebuilding phase."

The note of genuine embarrassment in her voice made him uneasy. "It's plenty classy. I've slept on the ground during cattle drives and in horse stalls on more than one occasion." By *slept,* he meant tossing and turning, trying to avoid nightmares of everything he'd lost.

Those hazel eyes locked on him, her expression inexplicably intense. "You work with livestock!"

Isn't that what he'd just said? "As often as I can." He preferred animals to people. "Sometimes I do other odd jobs, too. I was headed into Bingham Pass to get more information about a local employment opportunity."

"Then you haven't already committed to it?" A smile spread across her face, revealing two dimples. "Because, as it happens, *I'm* hiring." She stepped forward, extending her hand. The oversize jacket parted, revealing a still damp but not entirely transparent blouse. Thank God.

"I'm Hannah."

Hannah, Hazel. He'd been close.

"Hannah Shaw," she elaborated when he said nothing. "Owner of the Silver Linings Ranch."

Foreboding cramped low in his belly. Paralyzed, he neglected to shake her hand. "Not the Widow Shaw?" The one who baked cakes and harbored delusions of being a rancher?

She frowned. "People still call me that?"

Crap. It *was* her. He'd imagined Mrs. Shaw would be a temporary solution to his problems, but now, meeting her earnest gaze, his instincts murmured that she posed far more threat to his safety than any rifle-wielding jealous husband.

Chapter Two

"You know I'm rooting for you, but—"

"No *buts,* Annette." Hannah secured the phone between her ear and shoulder, needing both hands to separate the yolk from the egg white. "This is the answer to my prayers! Think about it—I've been scouring the county for a halfway-competent ranch hand, and one rides to my rescue on a rainy Wednesday evening? It's destiny."

Or, at least, proof that her positive thinking was finally—*finally!*—paying off. She executed a happy twirl, narrowly missing the antique buffet that served as a kitchen island. Though she'd been too excited to eat dinner after she'd showered off the road grime and changed into dry clothes, she was busy mixing a thank-you batch of devil's food cupcakes for Annette.

Over the past three months, Annette Reed had become like a big sister. Annette and her husband were trying to have kids; meanwhile they doted on Evan, helping create the extended family he'd never had. Annette was a blessing in their lives, even if she was slow to embrace Hannah's "bright side" philosophy. The other woman didn't fully understand that the determined optimism was the only thing that had kept Hannah going during the bleakest period of her life, that Hannah owed it to her son to prove good things *could* happen if you worked hard enough.

"Sweetie, please be careful," Annette entreated. "You wouldn't be the first woman in the world to get in trouble because she confused a hot guy on a motorcycle with destiny."

"Hot guy?" Hannah froze, glancing out the window into the dark, as if making sure Colin Cade couldn't overhear them. Which was insane since he was a quarter of a mile away, and she was locked into her house with a watchdog for company. "I never said he was hot."

"Not in so many words, but it was in your tone. What's he look like?"

Dark, with that shaggy, rich brown hair and unshaven jaw. Chiseled. And she didn't just mean the muscles outlined beneath his T-shirt. His features, though striking, looked as if they'd been carved from stone. Had the man ever smiled in his life? *Not that it matters.* Being charming wasn't a job requirement. She needed someone efficient and unflinching in the face of setbacks.

"He has blue eyes," she said noncommittally. Light blue with a hint of green. "And he's tall."

Her friend guffawed. "Next to you, sweetie, *everyone's* tall."

She ignored the crack about her height. "Annette, this isn't me getting my hopes up for no reason. The guy came here specifically looking for me, looking for this ranch." Granted, Colin had seemed more shell-shocked than enthusiastic when he'd realized he found her. "An old friend of Colin's told him I was hiring and he wanted more information." She'd kept her answers in the bunkhouse brief and cheerful, barely mentioning Henry White, the well-intentioned, semiretired ranch hand who came by at least twice a week.

"Did you tell him the truth?"

"More or less," she said, hearing the defensive note in her tone. "I mean, I didn't volunteer that today was my fifth bank meeting and that I got turned down again. I said that I'd inherited a family ranch, have plans to turn it into a cross between a small dude ranch and bed-and-breakfast but have yet to put together a staff." Unless one counted seventy-year-old Henry and his wife, Kitty. "I invited him to the main house for breakfast so we can discuss details. I'm making my homemade coffee cake."

"Ah. Pulling out the big guns, then."

Hell, yes.

As far back as Hannah could remember, she'd always had a plan. Her first one had been Get Adopted. That one had never worked out, but years later, for one shining moment in time, her marriage had made her part of a family. Eyes stinging, she batted away the memories and focused on the present. Current plan: rehabilitate the ranch that had been in her late husband's family, build it into a legacy for her son. And to do that, she needed Colin Cade.

She was a persistent woman looking to hire help, and he was a man with ranch experience who needed a job. A match made in heaven! How hard could it possibly be to convince him to stay?

"Good morning!"

Colin hesitated on the bottom step of the wraparound porch, momentarily stunned by Hannah's brilliant smile. And bright yellow peasant blouse. She would be murder on a man with a hangover.

As he'd mulled over the circumstances last night,

he'd tried to keep thinking of her as the Widow Shaw, but he couldn't reconcile that moniker with the woman who'd stepped outside of the two-story house to meet him. She looked as fresh as a spring morning with her feet bare, revealing hot-pink toenails, and her inky hair pulled high in a ponytail. If it hadn't been for the jeans she wore and the pair of muddy boots sitting on the porch, he would seriously question whether she actually owned this place.

Behind her, on the other side of the screen door, an unseen dog scrabbled against the metal lower half and barked. Hannah shushed the canine over her shoulder, then flashed another sun-bright beam in Colin's direction. "Don't worry, Scarlett doesn't bite. Come on in— breakfast is ready and waiting."

Even from outside the house, the food smelled too enticing, making his stomach growl in anticipation. He was reminded of the fairy tale he used to read his younger sister. *Hansel and Gretel.* Hannah's house might not be made out of candy, but temptation was present just the same.

Then again, she had a job to offer him. It was imperative that Colin stay busy. He needed physically draining, sunup-to-sundown work.

Resigned, he followed her through the front door. "Holy sh—" He broke off, manners belatedly overcoming his shock. "That's…some dog."

Hannah knelt down, patting the dog's head. "Meet Scarlett."

Yesterday, Colin had thought Hannah's truck an eyesore. Next to the dog, it was a luxury sedan. He'd seen "patchwork" mutts before with traits from different breeds that looked a little mismatched. Scarlett went beyond mixed-breed. She was FrankenDog. It was as if someone had placed a disproportionately large German shepherd head on a squat body—not an attractive head, either. The dog had a comically pronounced underbite and her ears weren't parallel. One black ear stood up atop her head, as was common with shepherds, and the other seemed to stick straight out of the side of her skull. What were the legs, basset hound? Her red-and-white coat couldn't decide whether it was supposed to be curly or straight, and her tail was a brindle-colored whip that didn't match anything else on her. He assumed her neck bolts were hidden beneath the bright blue collar.

"Scarlett," he echoed. He would've gone with "Hellhound," although that did imply a creature weighing more than forty pounds.

Hearing her name, the dog whined and smacked him with her wagging tail.

"She likes you. That's a good sign," Hannah declared as she stood, leading him through a spacious living room with a stone fireplace. He got a glimpse of a back hallway and a set of stairs, but she led him past that and into the kitchen. "I'm not a superstitious person, but everything about our meeting has been so lucky."

He kept his response to a vague grunt she could take either way. It was probably best not to argue with a potential employer, but mountainside storms and mutant dogs didn't strike him as auspicious omens.

"Hope you're hungry. I love to cook. Before I came here, I was a pastry chef."

"Big change."

"True, but I'd been studying ranches for years. Running this place was always the plan. Besides, I couldn't have stayed at my last job much longer." She scowled. "My boss—never mind. We should be eating," she chirped.

He was reluctantly fascinated by her total about-face. It was as though she'd flipped a switch. One moment, she'd clearly been remembering something unpleasant, anger seeping into her tone, then, boom, she was back to beaming like a lottery winner.

Maybe she was schizophrenic.

Aware that he was on the verge of staring, he looked away. In appearance, Hannah's kitchen wasn't much fancier than the bunkhouse. Chairs at the oblong table were mismatched, and the countertops bore stains and scratches. Faded wallpaper covered the spaces between appliances but had been scraped off the main wall, which was bare. However, the bounty on the island more than compensated for the modest surroundings. Crisp bacon; eggs scrambled with cheese, peppers and sausage; a bowl of fruit salad; piping-hot coffee; and a cake so moist it looked like the cover photo of some food magazine. His mind darted back to the *Hansel and Gretel* story and the witch who fattened up her prey.

He slanted Hannah an assessing look. "You got any ulterior motives I should know about?"

"Wh-what? You mean, like the old saw about the way to a man's heart being through his stomach? Because I am not interested in you! Not like that."

She sounded so vehement that he experienced a jolt of surprise. Maybe he was a few weeks—months?—overdue for a haircut, but he wasn't repulsive.

"I just wanted to make a good impression," she said. "I don't cook like this every morning, of course. Too many chores to be done. Although, we do splurge once a week, for Sunday breakfasts."

We? So far, he hadn't seen evidence of another person on this ranch.

Handing him a plate edged in feminine purple flowers, she nodded toward the food. "Dig in while the eggs are still warm. I'd love to discuss your references. Then after breakfast, I can give you a tour—"

She was cut off by Scarlett's frantic barking. The house rattled as the front door swung open with gale force. Hannah turned, an automatic smile blossoming as a child's voice hollered, "Mommy!" Then a little boy with a curly mop of hair nearly as dark as Hannah's skidded around the corner, launching himself at her in an exuberant hug.

Colin's heart clenched. The same delicious aromas that had been making his mouth water now turned his stomach. Nausea and memories boiled up inside him. Physically, the dark-eyed little boy didn't bear any resemblance to Danny, but he looked about the same age Danny would have—

"I have to get out of here." Addressing his words to no one in particular, he dropped his plate on the counter and strode toward the living room.

Colin's nerves had held steady while working with numerous wild-eyed horses too scared to realize he was trying to help; hell, he'd kept his cool during a stampede. But there were limits to his bravery. He couldn't be around kids.

He'd never taken a job where young children lived, and the Silver Linings Ranch would be no exception.

What just happened? Hannah was so stunned by Colin's announcement that it took her a moment to process his abrupt exit. This wasn't the first time someone had turned down her job offer, but none of the other candidates had actually bolted. She'd hit a new low in the interview process. "Wait!"

Gently disentangling herself from her son's sticky hug—was that jam on his fingers?—Hannah sprinted after Colin. And drew up short to avoid smacking into him. He, in turn, had apparently halted to avoid running over a startled Annette.

The blonde's mouth had fallen open in a perfect *O*, making her look like a comic strip character. "Um, hi?" Her eyes darted to Hannah. "Sorry, I...forgot you had a breakfast meeting."

Fat chance. Given the concern Annette had expressed over a stranger spending the night, Hannah wasn't surprised her friend had come over first thing to check on her. At least Annette hadn't dragged her husband, Todd, along. No doubt Annette had plenty of questions about why the man who should be sitting comfortably at the table listing his credentials had almost mowed her over.

Hannah stepped forward to make introductions—which just so happened to strategically place her between Colin and the front door. "Colin, meet Annette. She's here to drop off Evan and pick up some cupcakes. They're really good, if I do say so myself." Deep down, she hoped that if she kept talking, he couldn't leave. He might be gruff, but surely he wasn't brusque enough to walk out midconversation? "Annette, this is Colin Cade. We were about to eat and discuss Colin's previous ranch experience."

"No, we weren't," he said firmly. He gave a curt nod in Annette's direction. "Ma'am."

Annette raised a pale eyebrow. "Don't let me interrupt."

He shook his head, already moving toward the door again. Something in his demeanor suggested he would pick up Hannah and remove her bodily from his path if necessary. "Nothing to interrupt. I was on my way out." He opened the screen door, letting it clatter shut behind him.

Gesturing toward the kitchen in an all-purpose indication that Annette should help herself to the food and please keep an eye on Evan, Hannah followed. Was it her son's appearance that had sent Colin fleeing, or had she been too manic in her perky approach? One of her favorite high school teachers had always said that enthusiasm was contagious, but that didn't seem to be the case with Colin. Maybe she should dial it back a notch.

His much longer legs gave him the advantage. He was already down in the yard, but she wasn't too proud to jog down the porch steps.

"Wait, Colin, I—" *Crack.*

The board under her gave way, and Hannah gasped as her foot went through the fissure at a wrong angle. Suddenly, he was at her side, his hands warm on her hips as he lifted her. For a big man, he moved surprisingly fast.

"You're hurt." Putting his arms around her, he lifted her vertically so she wouldn't have to navigate the steps and lowered her onto the porch. Tingles of awareness erupted like goose bumps across her skin. It had been eternities since she'd been that close to a man.

"Twisted my ankle," she said breathlessly, "but it's nothing ice and ibuprofen won't fix."

He glowered, those blue eyes stormy. "You seem

to have some strange ideas about what's fixable. Your truck's a pile of scrap metal, and you live in a house that's rotting out from under you."

"It is not." Annoyed, she shoved away from him, not even caring that she had to hobble to do so. "I'll admit the steps need replacing—all the rain hasn't helped. Maybe some of the railing is a little loose, too. But I made sure the main house was structurally sound before I moved my son here."

At the mention of Evan, Colin's gaze skittered behind her, as if she'd reminded him that there was a nuclear warhead inside rather than a four-year-old boy.

"Wow. You really don't like kids, do you?"

He blanched, but didn't answer.

Admitting defeat, Hannah shook her head sadly. She was stubborn, not delusional. "Thank you for changing my tire yesterday. Safe journeys wherever you're headed next."

Trying to keep her weight off the throbbing ankle, she pivoted toward the door. With a sound of strangled frustration, Colin clamped his fingers around her upper arm.

"I don't know where I'm going next," he said through gritted teeth. "But I'm replacing those damn steps before I go." He glanced around the spacious wraparound porch. "This entire thing's probably a safety hazard that should be reinforced, if not rebuilt."

Renewed hope surged through her, eclipsing her pain. "I insist on paying for your time as well as the materials." She kept her voice calm, trying not to betray her joy at this small victory.

"You have tools?"

She nodded. "There's a small detached garage behind the house. Pretty well stocked, as far as I can tell. I can show you."

He slanted her an assessing glance. "You should get inside, off that ankle. If you've got a tape measure handy, I'll start taking measurements."

"Sure. I'll send Annette out with it. She can take you to the garage." Hannah made a mental note to instruct her friend not to interrogate Colin or overwhelm him with boisterous conversation. Otherwise, he might follow his original impulse and bolt. As it stood, she had at least a couple of days, a window of opportunity to plead her case. But with more subtlety this time.

He narrowed his eyes. "Just this one repair job. That's not the same as signing on with you, Mrs. Shaw."

She nodded innocently. *We'll see about that.*

Chapter Three

In the parking lot of a Bingham Pass diner, Colin sat inside a truck older than he was, as disoriented as if an Arabian Thoroughbred had kicked him in the skull.

Earlier that morning, he'd been ready to jump on his motorcycle and put Hannah Shaw, her energetic son and her ill-fated ranch all behind him. Yet he'd spent several hours purchasing lumber and paint and getting a new tire for her misbegotten truck. Since he'd never actually gotten around to eating breakfast—and because he was in no hurry to return to the Silver Linings—he'd stayed in town for lunch.

Bingham Pass, like his hometown of Cielo Peak, was rife with local gossip. As soon as Colin had mentioned the Silver Linings Ranch, the waitress had sighed sadly and remarked that Hannah's husband, a marine, had been killed overseas.

I was taught self-defense by a marine, and I'm a lot tougher than I look.

In hindsight, Colin acknowledged that his worry and anger at seeing Hannah fall through that bottom step had been disproportional to her minor injury. She seemed irrepressible. A mild sprain wouldn't keep her down for long. But how could he walk away, knowing a young woman or her kid might be hurt when he could have prevented it?

He couldn't leave with a clear conscience until he replaced the boards. Paradoxically, he still couldn't bring himself to return to the ranch yet—hence the sitting in a parked truck. He needed the few extra moments to brace himself for whatever surprise came at him next.

Ever since spotting Hannah through the rain, he'd felt off-kilter, unbalanced by her identity, her affable hellhound, the discovery that she had a little boy. None of it was what he'd expected. He should phone the so-called buddy who'd given him this lead. Colin had a few choice words for the man who'd led him to believe the "frail Widow Shaw" was a little old lady.

He powered up the cell phone he usually kept turned off. If asked, he would claim he left it off to make the charge last, but, truthfully, he was dodging his sister. A few weeks ago, Arden's husband had undergone major surgery in order to donate one of his kidneys to his biological father. As a concerned older brother, Colin had dutifully answered every one of her calls, wanting to be there for her in case anything had gone wrong.

But she'd abused the privilege. She'd acted as if she were calling with post-op updates on Garrett, but then she inevitably worked the conversation around to how Garrett's family could use the extra help on the Double F Ranch while he recuperated. Wouldn't Colin love the opportunity to use his skills on behalf of relatives and spend some time with his infant niece?

Colin knew his sister worried about him, that Arden wanted to help him heal. How could he explain that it hurt to be around her, the glowing new mother with a husband who adored her? Their brother, Justin, wasn't much better. He was engaged and disgustingly in love.

As soon as his phone finished booting up, it buzzed with the notification that he had 6 Missed Calls from Arden Frost. That was a lot even for her.

Fighting a stab of uneasiness, he dialed his brother Justin's number. If something were wrong, Justin would know. But if her calls were simply more attempts to recruit him to the Double F so she could keep an eye on him, then he was dodging a bullet by not phoning her directly.

It took a few rings before Justin answered. "Hey, old man. Long time, no hear. To what do I owe the honor?"

His brother's glib tone sent an unexpected stab of nostalgia through Colin. He hadn't seen either of his siblings since Christmas, which suddenly seemed like a long time considering how close they'd once been. Although there'd been an elderly aunt's name on the guardianship papers, Colin had all but raised his siblings after their parents' deaths.

He cleared his throat. "I, ah, wondered if you could tell me what our sister's been up to lately. She filled my voice-mail box. I figured it would be quicker to check in with you than listen to all of the messages. You know Arden. She's not brief."

Justin laughed. "Preaching to the choir. I realize it's a wuss move, but now that I'm engaged, I keep trying to make Elisabeth take her calls so I don't have to. Those two can talk wedding plans for *hours*."

Colin squeezed his eyes closed. Weddings, babies, new beginnings. It was difficult not to feel as if Arden and Justin were both just starting out in life while his had abruptly derailed. "So do you know why she's been calling me?"

Justin's heavy pause was worrisome. He usually had a quip for every occasion. "You should really ask her."

Colin's heart skipped a beat. Decades ago, they'd lost their mom to cancer and their father to heart failure. Had Arden inherited any medical problems? "Justin, you tell me right now, is she okay?"

"Relax, bro, it's *good* news." He sighed. "You didn't hear this from me, but she and Garrett are expecting."

"Again? Those two are like rabbits."

"Dude, it's only their second child."

"Yeah, but the first one's not even a year old! Shouldn't they be pacing themselves?"

"If it's all the same to you, I'd rather not think about our sister's sex life." Justin changed the subject. "How are things going with the McCoys?" His carefully neutral tone made it clear he'd heard something. Justin was no better at lying now than he had been as a kid.

"What do you know?"

"Only some very bizarre gossip about you and Delia McCoy. The ranching community talks. Garrett heard that you and Mrs. McCoy were caught in bed together, and he told Arden, who called me screeching. She didn't know whether to be relieved you're interested in a woman romantically or appalled that you'd be part of an adulterous affair."

Colin smacked his forehead. This was why he always left his phone off.

"Calm yourselves. Delia arranged to be caught in my bed, but I was nowhere near it. And I'm not interested in any woman." A pair of mesmerizing hazel eyes flashed through his mind, but no way in hell was he sharing that with his brother. "Look, I gotta go. I'll call Arden when I have more time to chat. I'll pretend to be surprised when she tells me about the baby."

"Gotta go where?" Justin pressed. "Are you still working at the McCoy place? Rumor has it you got canned, or is that part an exaggeration, too?"

Colin rolled his eyes heavenward, choosing his words carefully. If he admitted he was between jobs, he'd seem churlish and petty for not going home to visit his family. But all the Cades were forthright in nature. He was no more skilled at dishonesty than his brother. "I found a temporary gig on a spread in Bingham Pass." Very temporary.

"Glad you landed on your feet. Word of advice?" Justin asked, mischief lacing his voice. "Be careful not to make any goo-goo eyes at the boss's wife."

"I'm hanging up on you now. Also, the boss isn't married."

"Well, there's a relief."

The polar opposite, actually. Colin couldn't imagine anything less comfortable than working for an attractive single mom. Which was why, the second paint started drying on a newly secured porch, he was getting the hell out of Dodge.

When Scarlett worked herself into a frenzy by the front door, Hannah experienced an irrational burst of relief. *He's back.* It wasn't that she'd honestly believed Colin would steal her truck and never return. But he'd seemed so reluctant to be here that it would be good to see him with her own eyes, to have proof he was serious about staying for another day or two.

She got up from the kitchen table, where she'd been

paying bills on her laptop, and went to quiet the dog. As usual, indulgent "Aunt Annette" had let Evan stay up too late, and Hannah had sent her increasingly fussy son to take a nap. He'd been asleep only a few minutes.

But when Hannah saw who was on the other side of the screen door, instead of shushing Scarlett, she wanted to snarl right along with her.

"Afternoon, Hannah." Gideon Loomis tipped his gray felt cowboy hat, giving her a smile that would have been so much more handsome without the permanent smugness etched into his features.

Go away. "Gideon." It was tricky to avoid someone in Bingham Pass, downright impossible when that someone owned the neighboring ranch, but why was he standing on her front porch? After their lone dinner date, she'd tried to make it clear she wasn't interested in seeing him again. She'd stopped shy of blunt rudeness, because only an idiot would antagonize the Loomis family. "This is a surprise."

"A pleasant one, I hope." His self-assured tone made it clear he'd drawn his own erroneous conclusion. "Mama sent me over with an order for another one of her social events."

His mother, Patricia Loomis, was Hannah's biggest customer. There were decent restaurants in town that could cater, but no one in the area could bake or decorate desserts like Hannah. While she was thankful for Patricia's business, it also held her hostage. She longed for the freedom to tell Gideon he was an arrogant ass who was no doubt rendering himself infertile with his obnoxiously tight jeans.

Tugging on Scarlett's collar, she attempted to make the agitated dog sit. Scarlett had never liked Gideon, which proved the people at the shelter had known what they were talking about when they'd told Hannah the mutt was smart. She opened the door, grudgingly inviting her neighbor inside.

He inhaled deeply. "Always smells so delicious here. I just realized, I worked right through lunch. Don't suppose I could trouble you for a slice of cake and some coffee?" He was already making his way to the kitchen.

She ground her teeth together. "I don't have any coffee brewed." Since there was half a cake sitting in a clear domed container on the counter, she saw no polite way to refuse him that. She got a clean plate from the dishwasher and sliced a much smaller piece than she would have offered Annette. "We have to keep our voices down. Evan is sleeping. I was actually thinking about stealing the opportunity for a quick nap myself," she fibbed.

He ignored the hint that he should hurry on his way. "Sorry I missed the little guy. Be sure to tell him hi for me."

Evan didn't like Gideon any more than the dog did. For starters, the fiercely independent four-year-old, who couldn't wait for kindergarten, hated the "little guy" nickname. He also disliked how Gideon chucked him on the chin as if they were in some cheesy made-for-TV movie. Who did that in real life? One of Hannah's objections to the man was how he always seemed to be performing for an invisible audience.

She also objected to his barely concealed lust for her ranch.

Before she'd moved to Bingham Pass, she'd had ideas—and a budget—for guest-friendly investments. An outdoor hot tub, extra beds, more horses. But the six-bedroom ranch had fallen into disrepair since she'd seen it last, and she quickly realized she needed to prioritize roof improvements, furniture, updated plumbing and possibly even new wiring. Most of the outlets were only two-prong instead of the now-standard three. Alarmed by how inadequate her budget was, she'd let the Loomis family talk her into selling a strip of land that adjoined their property.

She'd regretted the hasty decision afterward, and not just because she'd realized they lowballed her on price. The Silver Linings Ranch was Michael's legacy to their son. She would not sell it off piecemeal like a stolen car stripped for parts. Gideon and his family weren't getting their hands on another acre of her land.

Aware of how easily her anger could grow—of the negative emotions that lurked like an undertow to consume her—she forced a smile. It was strained, but Gideon didn't seem to mind. He grinned back, leaning against the island to eat instead of going to the table as she'd hoped.

She found an excuse to move away from him, stepping toward the refrigerator. "Can I get you some iced tea? Maybe a glass of milk to wash down the chocolate?"

"Tea's fine." He took a bite of cake, and unmistakable bliss lit his brown eyes. "Damn, that's good. It's a crying shame you have to expend so much energy into taking care of the horses, cows and goats."

She didn't have goats. She was the proud owner of horses, cows and one attack donkey.

"If you had a husband to worry about the livestock for you," he continued, "think of all the extra time you could spend puttering in the kitchen and developing your recipes."

She straightened abruptly from the fridge shelf, skewering him with a glare. "Yeah, careless of Michael to get killed in action and screw up my *puttering* schedule."

"All I meant was—a woman like you? Deserves a man who can take care of her."

She wanted to rail that not only was she capable of taking care of herself, she'd been doing a splendid job of taking care of Evan for the past four years. Still… being a good mom and a hard worker didn't automatically translate to being able to maintain one hundred and eighty acres alone. *Not alone, exactly.* She had a four-year-old always looking for ways to "help." She also had Henry, who'd worked this property for decades and refused to acknowledge limitations set by age or reality, and Colorado's most unusual ranch dog.

Okay, she needed a man, but not in the romantic sense. Particularly if her options were limited to Gideon Loomis.

His expression earnest, he set down the plate and came toward her. "At the very least, let me talk to my folks about buying your cows from you. The herd would be one less thing for you to manage."

The "herd" was fewer than two dozen heifers, a bull and the resulting calves. Her predecessor, Michael's great-uncle, hadn't used a formal breeding program. He kept the bull in with the heifers, sometimes separating out the younger cows, and let nature take its course. A vet was called in as necessary, but the cattle were actually the least of her problems—with the exception of hauling hay. Hay was a never-ending chore.

"Isn't that sweet of you," she bit out, "offering to shoulder my burdens? No doubt for some sort of grateful, discounted rate."

His voice rose. "Are you accusing me of trying to cheat you? If you were a man…" He stopped, running a hand over his reddened face. His tone changed, slick with his attempt at charm. "But *you* are all woman."

"Maybe you're right, I do need a man." She jutted her chin up. "Good thing that, as of yesterday, I found one."

THERE WAS A shiny red pickup in front of the ranch house when Colin returned from town. When he'd left, Annette's car had been there. This must be someone different. He took the steps two at a time, glad Hannah had company. Maybe he could return the truck keys and get to work on the porch without further conversation. Even though she'd affirmed her understanding that he was sticking around only for this one quick repair job, did he really trust that she wouldn't try to coax him into staying?

More to the point, did he trust himself to resist? Home cooking like hers and the sibling-free solitude of the bunkhouse were appealing. If she didn't have a kid—or those arresting hazel eyes—he would have considered staying until his brother's wedding.

Before he had a chance to knock against the door frame, voices carried through the screen.

"—your sense? You can't just bring strange men home!"

"I told you to keep your voice down," Hannah retorted, her own voice only marginally softer. "And it's *my* ranch. I make the decisions. I think it's time for you to go, Gideon."

"I haven't finished," the man argued.

Not bothering to waste time knocking, Colin let himself inside, even as he called himself a fool. For all he knew, "Gideon" was a relative or a boyfriend and Hannah might resent a third-party interloper witnessing the argument. But Colin had a problem with the man's refusal to leave.

"Hannah?" He wheeled around the corner, distantly recognizing that it had been a long damn time since he'd felt protective of anyone but Justin or Arden.

His would-be boss was between the kitchen counter near the fridge and a beefy guy standing close enough that Colin had the urge to yank him back by his collar.

"You're back." Hannah's face went from tense to one of those dimpled smiles faster than a hummingbird could beat its wings. She raised an arm, pushing Gideon out of her way with the heel of her hand and coming to take the truck keys from Colin. "This is my neighbor, Gideon Loomis. He was just leaving."

The man's blond eyebrows shot toward the brim of his gray hat. "Actually, I—"

"Mommy?"

All three adults turned to see Evan in the wide entryway, his hair sticking up in wayward tufts, a child-size green blanket clutched in his hand.

Gideon gave the kid a hearty smile. "Oops—we wake you, little guy?"

Evan scowled.

"How about I make it up to you with a piece of cake?" Gideon offered.

"I don't think so." Hannah crossed the kitchen to scoop the boy up in a hug. "He had some after lunch.

No more sweets until after dinner. And only then if you eat some vegetables," she told her son.

Evan's wrinkled nose and unenthusiastic grunt nearly tugged a sympathetic smile from Colin. He himself was a meat-and-potatoes man. Natalie had always cajoled him to set a good example by eating more green stuff.

"If Danny doesn't see you eating food like broccoli or lima beans, he'll form a preconceived notion that they taste bad."

"That's not a notion—that's scientific fact."

Colin blinked, startled by the memory of teasing his wife. He was normally more vigilant about stifling those recollections. Dwelling on what he'd lost made it harder to move forward. *I need air.*

He cleared his throat. "I'm going to back the truck up to the garage and start unloading lumber. So…I'll be outside if you need me." The words were ostensibly for Hannah, but his gaze swung to Gideon. If Hannah asked her neighbor to leave again, Colin would be close enough to offer his assistance in escorting the man from the premises.

A few minutes later, as Colin stood on the porch double-checking some measurements, the front door opened. Hannah walked Gideon outside. She looked calmer, but her smile wasn't genuine. Her hazel eyes were flat, and no dimples showed.

Shaking his head, Colin rejected the involuntary sense of familiarity. He'd known Hannah for less than twenty-four hours. Who was he to assume he could read her?

"Please tell your mom I said thanks for the order," Hannah was saying. "And she's always welcome to call or email me. I hate for anyone to waste their time with an unnecessary trip."

There was a pause as Gideon digested her pointed words, and though Colin kept his eyes on what he was doing, he could feel the man's hostile gaze prickling the back of his neck like sunburn. "Wasn't any trouble. You've only been in Bingham Pass a few months, but we're neighborly around here. You'll come to realize there are a lot of benefits to that."

In Colin's experience, there were also benefits to being left the hell alone.

All Hannah said was, "Careful going down the stairs." She waited on the porch as Gideon climbed into his truck, expelling a frustrated breath as he pulled away from the house. "I swear, that man…"

When she didn't finish the thought, Colin turned toward her. She stood with her hands on her hips and her jaw tight.

"First my boss back in Colorado Springs didn't want to take no for an answer, and now Gideon with his macho I-know-best act. What is it about me that draws these yahoos? It's because I'm short, isn't it? Makes me look like an easy target."

His gaze slid down her body then back to her face, flushed with spirited indignation that made her hazel eyes sparkle like gemstones. "It's a lot more than your height that attracts men." What the devil was he thinking, saying that out loud? He'd spoken the truth, but there were too many wrong ways she could take his comment. She might lump him in with the inappropriate men she'd already been criticizing. Or, worse, she could take it as flirtation.

Colin didn't flirt. He left that to Justin, the glib charmer who'd set Cielo Peak dating records before asking Elisabeth to marry him.

Hannah looked momentarily startled by his words, but then nodded. "You're right, of course. Gideon's attracted to my ranch. I think his family looks at this property as the opportunity to expand their outfit. But I've got my own plans, which don't include the Loomises."

Right, her idea to remake the ranch as a B and B. In theory, he could picture her as the proprietor of a bed-and-breakfast. She seemed outgoing enough to make guests feel welcome and, though he'd yet to try her food, there was evidence suggesting her meals would keep tourists happy. But a friendly personality and impressive menu wouldn't be enough. For starters, she needed front steps that weren't lawsuits waiting to happen. Also, he was having difficulty imagining that abandoned bunkhouse as a guest cottage people would actually pay money to inhabit.

She grinned suddenly, exposing her dimples. "I can't tell if you're a *really* good listener, or if you're ignoring me in the hopes that I'll go away." She reached for the handle on the screen door. "I'll leave you alone so you can work, but thank you. Two rescues in two days—you're quite the hero."

Her praise slithered unpleasantly over him. The waitress in town had used that same word when talking about Hannah's late husband, a hero to his country. Colin was nobody's hero.

"You exaggerate my usefulness," he objected. "If I hadn't come along yesterday, you could have changed that tire without me. And as for today..." He recalled how close Gideon had been standing to her, looming.

How bad was the man's temper? Was he the type to lash out at a woman? "Do you think Gideon's a big enough problem that you needed rescuing?"

"You misunderstand. Today, *he's* the one you rescued." Hannah stepped inside, tossing one last beatific smile over her shoulder. "Another ten minutes with that blowhard crowding me, I might have Tasered his ass."

Chapter Four

Evan sat at the dinner table, rolling peas around his plate with his fork—as if his mom wouldn't notice he wasn't eating them as long as they stayed in motion.

"No peas, no dessert," Hannah reminded him gently. Rising, she carried her own plate to the sink.

Through the kitchen window, she could see Colin still working even though the sun had faded to an orange-gold memory stretched across the darkening horizon. She'd stepped outside nearly an hour ago to ask if he wanted to join them for dinner. It hadn't come as a surprise when he'd declined, asking only for a glass of water and for her to turn on the porch lights for more illumination. Granted, she didn't know him, but he seemed easiest in his own skin when he had a job to perform. So wouldn't it benefit them both if he stayed? Lord knew there was plenty to do around here.

Behind her, Evan heaved a martyrlike sigh. "Is this enough peas gone, Mommy?"

She grinned at his put-upon expression and the four remaining peas he was refusing to eat on principle. "I suppose so."

The town librarian had hired Hannah to bake some apple tarts for a fund-raising party, and she'd made extras to keep at home. She warmed one up and served it to Evan with a dollop of vanilla ice cream. Afterward, she settled him on the couch with Scarlett and "Train-ket," his beloved green train blanket. Having been washed hundreds of times, the fleecy material was no longer quite as soft as it had originally been, and the appliqué train was missing a car.

"I have to go down to the stable," she said, handing him a walkie-talkie so they could stay in communica-tion. Its match was clipped to her belt. Evan enjoyed feeling like a secret agent, and she couldn't imagine leaving sight of the house without being able to keep in contact. "You can watch cartoons until I get back. Then, bath time."

The first time she'd gone to the stable without Henry, Kitty or Annette to keep an eye on Evan, she'd been ner-vous. She didn't even like working in the garden without him, and that was within easy view of the house. They'd made a game of how he was a pirate and the sofa was his ship, and the carpet was shark-infested waters. But, truthfully, she allowed him so little television time that when she did, he was transfixed.

Before leaving the house, she stopped by the kitchen and sliced off a piece of the roast beef they'd had for dinner. She stuck it between two pieces of homemade bread, along with romaine, tomato and a dab of horse-radish. Then she wrapped it in a napkin and stepped onto the porch—where Colin was swearing in a cre-atively mixed string of words that reminded Hannah of a long-ago foster brother. Their foster mother had tried washing his mouth out a number of times, but then stopped, figuring that much soap wasn't good for a kid.

"Problem?" Hannah asked.

He turned to her, shoving a hand through his hair. She tried not to notice how lifting his arm like that tightened the white T-shirt against the muscular contours of his chest.

"I'm replacing some of the top boards on the porch so no one crashes through them like you did that step this morning, but it's not just the surface wood that needs fixing. Some of the supporting joists and piers are starting to give out, too. I'll need to make another supply run tomorrow."

Damn. Her budget was already strained, and porch repairs had not been on her priority list. That was the kind of thing she'd hoped to take care of once the bunkhouse was ready for guests and she'd had a chance to generate some revenue. *Bright side, Hannah.* If the scope of the job was greater than Colin had expected, then he'd be here longer, wouldn't he? That gave her a stronger chance of convincing him to help make her vision a reality.

With that in mind, she conjured a friendly smile and held out the sandwich. "I brought you some food."

He reached for it eagerly, but his eyes were wary. "What, just one course?"

Maybe now wasn't the time to mention the six different dessert options inside if he was still hungry later. "I can do understated," she said. "I told you this morning, the kind of spread I laid out for breakfast is indicative of special occasions. Not a daily occurrence."

He scowled, looking uncomfortable at being classified with "special occasions," but then he took a bite of the sandwich. For a second, his features relaxed into an expression of utter satisfaction, and everything female in her clenched at the sight.

Partly out of self-preservation and partly in strategic retreat, she grabbed the now-empty glass of water and went back inside to get him a refill.

"Mommy?" Evan said as she entered the room. "I've seen this one before."

She changed the channel and found him a different cartoon. "I have to give Mr. Colin some water, then I'm going to feed the horses. For real this time," she said, ruffling his dark hair. Evan had her hair and eye color, but Michael was the one who'd had curls as a child. Plus, Evan had his father's smile.

When she returned to the porch, she found Colin packing away tools for the night.

She sat on the bench, tugging on her boots. "Can I ask you a favor? I mean, besides the obvious one you're already doing, rebuilding my disaster of a porch? I was headed to the stable and wondered if you'd come with me. I know you've had more experience with livestock than me, and I'd really appreciate your expert opinion on the horses. Not that Henry isn't an expert, but…"

He cocked his head in silent question. She was used to the chatter of her inquisitive son and Henry's garrulous tales of bygone days. Colin didn't waste a lot of words.

"Henry White," she said. "He worked this ranch for years, and he knows his stuff. His eyesight isn't what it used to be, though, and he's a little more, um, absent lately. I'm learning as fast as I can, but I can't guarantee that if Henry overlooked something I would catch it."

Colin pressed a finger between his eyes, and she could almost see his thoughts floating in the cool evening air. *This lady doesn't know what she's doing. Can't she see this is a doomed enterprise?* She refused to believe that. No one was born an expert at anything. What message would she be sending her son if she gave up whenever she encountered difficulties?

She thought back to her conversation with Colin in the bunkhouse. "You said you work with animals 'as often as you can.' You must care about their well-being."

He sighed. "Lead the way."

"Thank you." Turning so he wouldn't see her victorious grin, she opened the container beneath the porch bench and pulled out a large flashlight. There was enough light to get to the stable, but it would be darker when they came back. She stepped gingerly down the stairs. "You can use the flashlight for your walk to the bunkhouse tonight. Or I could drive you."

"Walking's fine," he said. "It isn't far to the bunkhouse, and I'm not afraid of the dark."

She almost made a joke about her son and his various coping mechanisms for braving the dark but stopped herself. Colin hadn't warmed to Evan. She wished it didn't bother her—tried to tell herself his aloofness was better than Gideon's phony "let's be best pals" demeanor—but she was a mom. She naturally wanted others to see what a great kid Evan was.

"How's your ankle?" Colin asked as they fell into step in the yard.

"Better. Tender, but—"

"Mommy!" Evan called through the screen a moment before banging the door open. He was wearing his own pair of boots and had his blanket around his shoulders like a superhero cape. "Changed my mind. I wanna visit the horsies, too."

Repressing a groan, she stole a peek at Colin. He looked as if he'd swallowed rusty nails.

It was on the tip of her tongue to tell her son no, but the whole reason she'd been comfortable leaving Evan for a short time was because she'd trusted him to watch TV. That obviously wasn't going to work tonight. Apparently, the combination of horses and a newcomer to their ranch was a lot more mesmerizing than watching Shaggy and Scooby unmask villains.

Colin met her gaze. "Makes no difference to me," he said stiffly. But, in direct contradiction to his words, he lengthened his stride, putting distance between himself and the Shaws.

"Come on," she told her son. She pointed at the broken step. "Be careful, though."

Evan scampered down the stairs with no care for his safety, rushing by Hannah and going straight to Colin. "You're tall." Her son's voice was full of admiration. "You're like a *giant*."

Unsurprisingly, Colin didn't answer. The silence didn't deter Evan.

"Did you get tall from eating healthy food? Mommy sings me a song about—"

"Evan!" She intervened before her son reenacted the "Grow Big and Strong" song she'd made up to coax him into eating vegetables. Colin didn't need to hear it—or see the accompanying dance steps. "Don't bother Mr. Colin, okay? He's been working with a noisy saw and hammering nails all afternoon. I'll bet he'd appreciate some peace and quiet."

Her son scowled. "Quiet is *boring*."

"Don't argue with your mother." Colin's sharp admonishment wasn't loud, but it startled both Evan and Hannah. She hadn't expected him to speak. Having him suddenly participate in the conversation was otherworldly, like being riddled by the sphinx.

Evan's eyes were wide as he craned his head back to regard the "giant." "Yessir." Then he miraculously fell silent.

Hannah was impressed. She'd wanted Colin to stick around because of his experience with livestock, but it turned out he wasn't half-bad with outspoken four-year-olds, either. She caught up with him, turning to give him a smile of thanks. It died on her lips, though, when she got a good look at his profile. Even in the dim light of moonrise, there was no mistaking the pain stamped across his handsome features.

It was an expression that felt familiar, the same kind of agony that had contorted her soul when she'd lost both her husband and, in the same day, her mother-in-law. Ellie Shaw hadn't been well, and news of Michael's death had triggered a massive stroke. After years of foster care and praying for home and family, Hannah had lost her only two relatives in one cruel blow. A week later, Hannah had gone into premature labor, barely caring when she was loaded into the ambulance whether she lived or died.

It wasn't until the next day, when she'd heard Evan's lusty wail, that she'd realized a piece of Michael still lived on, that not all her family was dead. She had a son who needed her, and she was ashamed of her earlier ambivalence about surviving. For his sake, she'd sworn to find the positives in life, to resist the bleak drag of depression that sucked at her. Evan was the bright spot that motivated her to keep moving forward during the most challenging times.

What motivated Colin Cade? And what had he suffered? She'd never seen such light eyes filled with so much darkness.

COLIN BREATHED IN the familiar scents of leather and wood, horse and hay. They were soothing, but as ragged as his nerves were after walking to the stable with Hannah and her boy, he would have preferred a slug of whiskey. It was weird how being around kids stirred memories not only of his own lost son, but his father, who'd died when Colin was a teenager. *Don't argue with your mother.* How many times had Colin heard that edict from behind the newspaper at the kitchen table, directed either at himself or Justin, who'd been a rambunctious hellion as a kid? When Dad bothered to lower the newspaper before making the pronouncement, you knew you were *really* on thin ice.

Was it strange to miss his parents after all this time? Colin's mom had been dead now for more years of his life than she'd been alive. But it was easier to miss them than to allow himself to miss Natalie and Danny. That was a more recent wound, one that hadn't healed properly. He could almost envision the jagged scar it had left inside him.

After the cover of darkness outside, being beneath the stable's electric lights made him feel too exposed, as if Hannah would be able to glimpse into his memories. He cleared his throat, shifting focus on the horses that had begun to wander into stalls from the outside paddock.

"Guess they know it's dinnertime," he said. "How many horses are there?" There were a total of eight spacious stalls, and the stable was in better shape than either the main house or his current quarters. Whoever had owned the ranch before, decor hadn't been his or her top priority.

"Four. Mavis here is the oldest," she said, coming forward to stroke the nose of a sorrel mare. "She's been on the ranch for seventeen years. I take her out for exercise, but when this place is up and running, I don't plan to let guests ride her. There's Tilly and Apples, both Tennessee walkers and good with people. Viper's the black gelding. He's a little sneaky, but doesn't challenge confident riders."

She showed Colin where the oats and feed buckets were. They hung them over the stall doors and snapped them into place. He noticed that the wood at Viper's stall had been chewed.

"That may be an indication that he needs more roughage," he commented. "Might want to give him more hay before he fills up on the oats."

Evan was suitably quiet and restrained around the horses. Hannah had obviously taught him stable manners. Or he was intimidated by the thousand-pound beasts. He eyed them with a combination of adoration and apprehension.

"We have a donkey, too," Evan informed Colin. "His name is Ninja."

Hannah took her son's hand and gently led him out of the stall where Colin was running a brush over Apples, getting to know the horse and checking her general condition. "I laughed the first time Michael told me donkeys were used to help protect the cattle against predators." She bit her lip. "Michael was my husband."

"The marine." He met her gaze, understanding the relief he saw there. She was glad he already knew, sparing her any awkward explanations. "I heard about him in town."

According to Colin's waitress, Michael had been killed before his son was born. Hannah's late husband had never seen Evan drag his green blanket across the dusty floor or heard his son ask when he would be big enough to ride a horse all by himself. *At least I had two years with Danny before he was ripped away.* But in some ways, wasn't that worse? There were still nights Colin woke from dreams of the past with the sound of his toddler's surprisingly deep belly laugh echoing in his ears.

"Last month, I watched Ninja circle up the cows with the youngest of the herd in the center," Hannah continued. "I never got a look at what they were reacting to—"

"Coyotes, probably."

She nodded. "The incident gave me a new appreciation for donkeys as unexpected heroes."

There was that word again. She'd called him a hero earlier, and he'd bristled, resenting the implied expectations that came with such lofty praise. But if she was comfortable using the same terminology when describing a donkey, maybe Colin should relax and get over himself.

It was a radical thought.

While Hannah and Evan stepped outside to see if they could find the Big Dipper, Colin tried to recall the last time he'd been relaxed. In the weeks following his brother's engagement Colin had figuratively held his breath, afraid that Justin—notorious for being unable to commit—would somehow screw up the best thing that had ever happened to him. Though Colin didn't spend much time in Cielo Peak these days, the habit of worrying after his siblings was tough to break. He should have been at ease during his last few ranch jobs, doing work he enjoyed, but circumstances such as Delia McCoy's unwanted interest had prevented that from happening.

Well, you won't find contentment here. Not with Evan looking for opportunities to talk his ear off and the losing battle of trying to help Hannah turn the run-down house into a tourist destination. Yet even as Colin reminded himself of the reasons he wasn't staying, he had to admit that right now, in this quiet stable, he was experiencing the closest thing to peace he'd felt in longer than he could remember. And he was in no hurry to give that up.

Chapter Five

"So you're the fella lookin' to replace me?" The grizzled man slammed his truck door, and Scarlett ran down the steps to greet him, woofing happily.

Colin set down the hammer and rose, deciding this must be Henry White. The man wore a battered straw cowboy hat that looked a lot like the one atop Colin's own head. "Not sure what you heard, sir, but I'm not replacing anyone. Are you Henry White?"

"Yup." The man's demeanor was so territorial, Colin was surprised it had taken him until Saturday to come size up the perceived competition. "Been working this ranch since before you were born."

As Colin understood it, that was part of the problem. But he had a lot of respect for what could be learned from previous generations. "I'm Colin Cade. Just passing through Bingham Pass and lending Hannah a hand while I'm here."

The man nudged back the brim of his hat. "Lotta people seem eager to help Hannah. Gideon Loomis, for one."

Was he trying to warn Colin away, let him know Hannah was spoken for? *She deserves better.* "Met Loomis. Wasn't impressed."

Henry's craggy, sun-leathered face split into a grin. "Me, neither. His parents may run a successful operation, but their spoiled only child doesn't have the sense God gave a goose."

So Colin had passed a test of sorts. The approval was oddly satisfying, and he found himself returning the old-timer's smile.

"Oh, good, you're here," Hannah called from inside the house. "I—" She stepped onto the porch, then froze, gaping at Colin. She looked so feminine in the white lacy sundress, a dramatic contrast to her shining black hair, that it wouldn't have been a hardship to stand there staring back at her. Over the past couple of days, he'd gotten used to seeing her in jeans and periodically dotted with flour or melted chocolate.

"Something wrong?" He glanced over his shoulder, trying to see if he'd overlooked a glaring mistake. None of the local stores carried the exact decorative spirals that were part of the porch railing, so after consulting the budget with Hannah yesterday morning, they'd decided to alternate. He'd found reasonably priced, complementary balusters and was installing the new ones in a pattern, salvaging as many of the former ones as possible. He was almost ready to paint.

"N-no. Nothing's wrong. I just…You were *smiling*. I didn't think that was possible," she said under her breath.

The observation left him self-conscious. *I smile*. Occasionally.

"I see you've met Henry," she said. "He's going to watch Evan while Annette and I visit an estate sale I've had on my calendar. I'm really optimistic about finding some furniture for the bunkhouse!"

As far as he could tell, "really optimistic" was her default setting. But today her enthusiasm was contagious.

"Best of luck," he said. He even threw in another smile for good measure.

She blinked, but then collected herself. Her dimples flashed in a mischievous smirk. "Warn me next time you're going to do that so I can put on my sunglasses."

He chuckled at that, the sound rusty even to his ears.

Then they were both distracted by Evan joining them on the porch. Hannah explained that the boy was in the middle of lunch and there was plenty of leftover spaghetti in the pot if Henry or Colin wanted some. Colin was always grateful when she brought him food outside, but so far he'd managed to avoid joining her and Evan for meals. Henry, however, had no such reservations about pulling up a chair at the kitchen table.

"I came hungry," he said. "I know better than to eat before setting foot in your house. God knows I love Kitty, but her cooking can't hold a candle to yours. Don't ever tell her I said that," he added, looking suddenly alarmed.

Hannah mimed crossing her heart. "Your secret's safe with me."

Evan was bored with the discussion of spaghetti. As he threw his slim arms around Henry's legs in a welcoming hug, he demanded, "Are we going fishing today?"

"That depends on how good you are and whether Henry feels up to it," Hannah said sternly. "Don't pester him about it. And if the two of you do go, you have to exit through the back door. This area will probably be covered with wet paint."

He'd done a few boards in the garage last night so that they'd be dry and people could have a pathway through the front door, but he didn't trust the four-year-old to stick to the path. After blowing his mother a kiss goodbye, Evan led Henry inside, talking a mile a minute about the size of the fish he was going to catch.

Hannah watched them go, laughing softly. "Our pond is stocked with trout, but to hear him talk, you'd think we had marlin in there. Henry is good with him—with any luck, you won't even notice they're here. But if you need anything, my cell number is on the fridge. So is Kitty's. She and Henry live just down the road, so she can be here in a matter of minutes. A lot faster than me."

Especially if Hannah ended up with a flat tire or some other roadside emergency. "You're taking the truck?" he asked.

"It has a lot more cargo space than Annette's car and pulls the trailer better. I figured it was best to plan for a big haul. Power of positive thinking and all that."

He opened his mouth to comment, then thought better, shaking his head.

"What?" Her hazel eyes narrowed. "Were you about to make some snide comment about my truck?"

"About you. Not snide," he backpedaled. "I was just wondering if this is something you were born with or a learned behavior—your sunny disposition, I mean. Does everyone in your family see the world in such a rose-colored view?"

She jerked her head away abruptly, reaching into her purse and pulling out the sunglasses she'd mentioned. When she turned to face him again, the dark-tinted frames obscured her expression. "I was an orphan, actually."

They'd both lost their parents? The revelation of more common ground threw him for a loop. He and Hannah Shaw were polar opposites. He wouldn't have guessed that their backgrounds shared many similarities.

"Your parents are dead?" he heard himself ask.

"I honestly have no idea. Never met them," she said matter-of-factly. "I was abandoned as a newborn and grew up mostly in foster care. But to answer your question, the 'sunny disposition' was self-taught. I suppose I could moan and sulk my way through life, being bitter about anything that went wrong, but what kind of example would that be for my son?"

Her words had an edge to them. Because the topic was upsetting for her, or because she'd taken his question as criticism?

Or was *she* perhaps criticizing *him?* Colin may not have been flashing smiles left and right for the past three days, but he sure as hell wasn't sulking.

"I should go," she said briskly. "Annette is sacrificing most of her Saturday for me. It would be rude to keep her waiting."

He didn't like watching her go, her posture rigid as she climbed into the cab. He'd wanted to say something else, but nothing came to mind. *Goodbye* would have been insultingly trite after she'd shared something so personal, and *I'm sorry* felt like overkill when he wasn't even sure why he'd be apologizing.

It wasn't until the truck disappeared from sight that words formed in his mind, belatedly shaping the questions he wanted to ask. *How?*

How do you do it? Where do you find the strength?

But the sentiments were difficult to even think. There was no chance he'd be voicing them aloud.

No matter how much he ached for the answers.

"I HAVE TO hand it to you." Annette spoke over the hard rock station that was Hannah's guilty pleasure. There were a lot of songs she enjoyed listening to that weren't Evan-friendly. So she indulged in suggestive lyrics and some heavy metal when he wasn't riding with her. Annette paused. "You mind if we turn this down?"

Yes. The angry-sounding electric guitar riff suited her temper. "Of course not." Hannah reached for the volume knob. Annette was a fantastic friend and didn't deserve to bear the brunt of Hannah's dark mood. *Damn cowboy.* She'd stepped out of the house in such an upbeat mood and seeing Colin's smile—as rare and awe-inspiring as a unicorn—had seemed like an omen of good things to come. And then it had all gone down the crapper.

Annette started over, her tone admiring. "As I was saying, I'm impressed. I thought you were crazy, bringing home some stranger off the road to solve your problems—especially when it seemed like he didn't want to be there. But somehow you've kept him there."

"It's not like I took him hostage," Hannah grumbled. "He's free to leave anytime he wants." Hell, he could be packed up and gone when she got back and she wouldn't care. Except, of course, she would because the front deck had never looked better and he was great with the horses. She'd followed up with an acquaintance of an acquaintance, the man who'd sent Colin her direction in the first place, and she'd been surprised to learn he'd once been a veterinarian. Large animal vets made a nice living. What was a guy with experience like that doing fixing her porch? *Besides making me crazy.*

"Han? You okay?"

"Fine."

"Uh-huh. You do realize we're doing fifteen miles over the speed limit?" Annette asked cautiously.

Whoa. Hannah immediately eased off the accelerator, embarrassment washing through her. "Sorry."

"Let's try this again, but with you telling me the truth this time. What's wrong?"

Hannah sniffed, mortified to discover that her eyes stung. What was wrong with her? So Colin thought she was some naive Pollyanna with an unrealistic view of the world. What did that matter? He'd made it clear he wasn't sticking around. In the greater scheme of her life, he was barely a footnote. His opinion didn't count.

Except that part of you wonders if he's right. No one thought she could do this—not smug Gideon, not any of the loan officers she'd talked to, not even her best friend, who was on her side.

"Annette, is there a specific part of my plan that you think will cause me to fail? Or is it just that you believe the entire endeavor is doomed?"

"Oh, sweetie, I've been a terrible friend, haven't I? Whenever I call you in tears over starting my latest period, you're there for me, making me laugh and assuring me Todd and I will become parents eventually. But I haven't supported you."

"You've been there for me in tangible ways—helping with Evan, coming with me today." Annette's husband, Todd, who worked out of a home office at their farm as an accountant, had also offered lots of concrete help, giving Hannah monetary advice and going over all of the ranch's financial information.

"I know your skepticism stems from concern," Hannah added. "But…"

"But you need to feel like someone's in your corner? I am so sorry. I'm a hypocrite. I can't stand the idea of you facing any disappointment, yet being disappointed month after month hasn't stopped *me* from trying to get pregnant. You should follow your dream. I mean, this conversation started with me being impressed. More and more people are coming up to me in town wanting your contact information to order baked goods, and when I swung by yesterday to drop off the eggs, I could tell the porch is going to look great when it's finished. If you and Colin can work that magic on the inside of the house—"

"He still hasn't committed to staying once the project is finished," Hannah admitted. "I was getting the impression that he'd changed his mind, but it's not official."

Annette shrugged. "He clearly doesn't have anywhere he needs to be, or he'd be there already. If the two of you are getting along and you can afford to pay him, why leave?"

Hannah nibbled at her lower lip. Her friend's reasoning was logical, but the "getting along" part might be more complex than Annette realized.

"I snapped at him before I came to pick you up."

"You? Your version of snapping is probably different from most people's. You have the patience of a saint."

"No, I don't. I'm no saint. I'm an extremely stubborn woman who masks her stubborn streak with a smile."
Speaking of which...

She flipped back to that mental photo she'd captured of Colin's smile. Damn, the man was sexy. She'd known that already, of course. Her kitchen window overlooked the porch. She'd had a front-row view of him flexing muscles beneath thin cotton T-shirts damp with sweat. However, she'd assumed his hotness was limited to that brooding, Heathcliff kind of appeal. Today, he'd blown that hypothesis right out of the water. If he leveled that grin against a woman with intent, there was no telling what he could charm her into—or out of.

"So what caused you to snap at him?" Annette asked. "Is it the way he treats Evan?"

Actually, his tolerance of the boy seemed to have increased. He was never going to hand the kid a toy tool set and ask for his help, but he seemed to have fallen into the habit of letting Evan blather while he worked. He didn't engage, but neither did he cringe anymore whenever her son got within twenty feet of him.

"He insinuated I see the world through rose-colored glasses, and it didn't sound like a compliment. Plus, he asked about my family," she added heavily. She didn't need to elaborate. Annette had heard all about her history over a bottle of wine shortly after Hannah moved to Bingham Pass.

When Michael's father died during their first year of marriage, she'd taken it nearly as hard as her husband. The Shaws were the family she'd always craved. Mrs. Shaw had said later that at least he'd lived to see the wedding. Those words had haunted Hannah when Ellie died before seeing her grandson born. If she'd been able to hold Evan in her arms, would it have helped mitigate the loss of her son enough that she could cope? That she might have survived?

But there was no way to know that, and no way to change the past. All Hannah could do was keep working toward the future. And she would do it with or without Colin Cade's assistance.

COLIN REALIZED TWO things simultaneously—first, he was *starving;* second, he no longer heard any noise from inside the house. Earlier, Henry and Evan had been playing some game that consisted of rolling lots of dice at once. The clang of dice rattling together in a cup had been somewhere between maracas and machine gun fire. But Colin had become so absorbed with the paint job that he hadn't noticed when the din stopped. Apparently, they'd gone out the back for their fishing expedition without his even realizing it.

Since he couldn't tackle a second coat until the first dried, he was at loose ends. And Hannah had invited him to help himself to some food. Though he'd been avoiding entering the house unless absolutely crucial, the thought of microwaving a bowl of spaghetti made his stomach growl. It wasn't as if he'd be disturbing anyone. He crossed quickly through the living room, passing the high-backed couch and absently registering that the laminate floor looked pretty good. Hannah had replaced the carpet this week. She'd said she didn't have money for real hardwood, but she wanted that homey, rural effect.

Her plan was to renovate the bunkhouse and common areas first—kitchen, living room, deck—so that she could open for limited business, then tackle the four upstairs guestrooms as incoming funds allowed. He understood the logic, but he wasn't sure visitors would be able to enjoy a hearty lunch or read peacefully by the fireplace while construction was going on overhead.

His first sight of the kitchen impressed him even more than her replacing the floor on her own, minus his negligible contribution of cutting some pieces for her in the garage. Last time he'd been in here, she'd still been in the process of stripping wallpaper. Now the walls gleamed a pale yellow that looked like sunbeams, dotted with thin ribbons of royal blue. The only downside was that, against the shiny new wall coverings, the chairs and table looked even shabbier. But what did he know? She'd probably be home in an hour or so with a perfect set.

He'd spent the past few days marveling at her faith that things would always work out, but the interior of her house was proof that Hannah wasn't operating on blind faith. She was busting her ass to make things happen. She was juggling orders from townspeople, raising Evan, tending the garden, redecorating... When did she sleep? How did she replenish her energy so that she had enough left to deal with her spirited son, an aged, cantankerous ranch hand and a newcomer who was so surly that he apparently hadn't smiled a single time in three days?

The oregano-laced aroma of spaghetti sauce drew him from his musings and reminded him of his purpose. He was punching buttons on the microwave when he heard an odd thump. From somewhere above him? Maybe a critter on the roof or in the attic. But when the second thump came, he revised his opinion. That would be an awfully big critter. *Scarlett.* The dog was in the house somewhere, so—

Wait a minute. The dog was in the kitchen with him, sitting patiently next to the counter and watching with expectant brown eyes, drool forming at the corner of her mouth. Living with a kid, she was probably accustomed to plenty of food being dropped for her enjoyment.

"Hello?" Colin called. Maybe Hannah was back from her shopping expedition.

Curious, he retraced his steps to the living room. This time, he rounded the sectional sofa, which sat with its back to the kitchen, to get a better look. Henry was asleep on the couch, a DVD case covered with superheroes in his hand and a mostly empty bowl of popcorn kernels on his chest.

"Henry?" Colin shook the man's arm. The babysitter muttered in his sleep, but didn't wake.

Colin winced in realization. The thumping was Evan unsupervised somewhere in the house—hopefully in his own bedroom, where he was doing nothing more hazardous than circling toy trains over a plastic track. But the noise had sounded as if it came from above. He strode quickly toward the back hallway. What kind of shape were those upstairs rooms in? What items were stored there that might be equal parts fascinating and dangerous to a little boy? Having watched Hannah with her son, he doubted she'd intentionally leave anything like matches or power tools in plain sight or easy access, but—

"What are you doing?" The shout erupted before Colin could contain himself, and he bolted toward the top of the stairs just in time to throw his arms around the kid and keep him safely on the landing.

Evan gave him one wide-eyed look of surprise, then burst into tears.

Okay, that probably hadn't been the best way Colin could have handled the situation. He took a deep breath, making a concerted effort not to raise his voice again or shake the boy by the shoulders. It wasn't unheard of for a child to attempt sliding down a banister, but *headfirst?* That would have been a terrible idea even if the railing weren't rickety and led straight to a sharp-edged newel that looked capable of putting an eye out.

"Evan?" Henry's voice came from below, groggy and filled with concern.

When Colin turned to answer, "He's up here," Evan took the opportunity to scamper around him and dart down the steps. During his escape, the ever-present train blanket fluttered from his shoulders and landed on the staircase. It was evidence of the kid's panic that he didn't return for it.

Colin met a shame-faced Henry at the bottom of the stairs.

"I screwed up," the other man said. "We were watching a movie, and I guess I dozed."

"No harm done." What would be the point in Colin telling the man about how Evan had been about to take a dive down the balustrade? It had scared a year off Colin's life, and Henry needed all the years he had left. "But I think I startled him. I don't know about you, but I could use some coffee. Would you mind starting a pot while I go have a talk with him, man to man? I reckon you know where Hannah keeps all the coffee stuff. She talks about you like you're family."

The man's hunched shoulders rolled back as pride lit his expression. "Happy to brew some. But it'll be good old-fashioned regular coffee. I ain't using that fancy cappuccino thing she brought with her from Colorado Springs."

Henry shuffled off to the kitchen, and Colin walked down the hallway. In the front areas of the house, perhaps because they were still being decorated or maybe because Hannah hadn't wanted to make them too personal, he hadn't seen many family pictures. But hanging on the long wall that ran between the stairs and the downstairs bedrooms were a dozen portraits in different styles and sizes. Most were of Evan, a few showed him with his mother, but the largest was Hannah and Michael's wedding picture.

He didn't *want* to look at it, didn't want to put a face to the hero husband she'd lost. Didn't want to look at the joy she radiated as a bride and think about how devastated she must have been to receive the news of Michael's death. Why was it so hard to glance away? And why couldn't he separate where her imagined pain stopped and his pain began? He'd had his own smiling bride, once, and thoughts of all he'd wanted for Natalie were like acid burning through him. If it had been within his power, he would have given her the world. *I miss you, Nat.* He hardly ever let himself think the words, but the truth of them was always there, beneath the surface.

If she were here, she'd know what to say to a startled four-year-old who'd just been busted. Natalie had been a people person. He could almost hear her in his head. *The kid thinks of you as a giant. Imagine how scary you must look to him.*

At the end of the hall were two bedrooms opposite each other, with a shared bathroom between them. To the left, he glimpsed a neatly made queen-size bed with a pale purple and dusky-blue comforter. He abruptly turned away. On his right, there were sounds of sniffling. He followed them into a room decorated with primary colors that were bright enough for the circus. The sniffling came from inside a red-and-yellow pup tent in the corner of the room.

"Hey." Colin knelt in front of the zipped flaps. "Can I come in?"

There was a pause on the other side of the nylon. "Y-you won't fit. Too big."

"Guess you're probably right about that. Can you come out then? I brought your blanket."

There was a metallic whirr as the zipper teeth parted. A skinny arm shot out. Colin handed over the blanket, and the arm disappeared back inside the tent. Hard to say whether this could be considered progress. *At least he didn't rezip the door.*

Colin peeked through the opening but didn't stick his head inside, giving the kid his space. "What were you doing on the stairs?"

"I wanted to fly." Evan twisted his blanket in his hands. "I know I can't—not for-real flying—but I had on my cape and wanted to go fast."

"You would have gone fast, but you probably would've fractured some bones in the process. That's why I yelled, because I was so worried about you."

"Yelling's mean." The sniffing started again. "You *scared* me."

"If it makes you feel better, I think you scared me more." The fool kid could have broken his neck. Colin's stomach churned. "The thought of telling your mom that something had happened to you… She would be—" Emotion swelled in his throat, making it impossible to speak. But, really, what could he say? There were no adequate words for what parents suffered when they lost a child.

"Mr. Colin?" Evan's voice was hesitant, but close.

Colin jerked his head up, realizing Evan had partially emerged from his sanctuary.

"Are you gonna cry?"

"What?" Surprised by the question, Colin raised a hand to his eyes, realizing his vision was beginning to blur. Dammit. He looked back at the curious little boy, but for a moment, he didn't see Evan Shaw. He saw Danny's face. Danny laughingly demanding to be swung high in the air. Danny, solemn as he nodded his understanding that the oven was hot and that he needed to stay back. Danny worn out after a Christmas carnival, asleep on his stomach with his little butt curved in the air.

That now-familiar suffocating sensation crowded Colin's chest. He shot to his feet, wanting to put as much space as possible between himself and this room filled with all the bright adventure of childhood.

"Wait." Evan followed him, and even though Colin's goal had been to coax the kid out, now he wished the boy would stay away from him. "Do you need Trainket?"

The innocent, heartfelt gesture sliced through him. His throat felt as if it was on fire, but he managed to say, "Thanks, kid." They stood there for long minutes, Colin clutching a grubby green blanket and Evan staring up at him, probably mystified by what could be so awful that it would make a mean old giant teary.

"Mr. Colin? Are you going to tell Mommy what I did?"

Keeping secrets was a bad idea. On some level, Colin knew that. It forged a bond between them that he wanted no part of, plus it might undermine Hannah as a parent. But he neither wanted to rat the kid out, nor scare Hannah with what could have happened. "How about I make you a deal? I'll build you your own headquarters—all the great superheroes have a special place they can go."

"Like my tent?" Evan interrupted.

"Bigger. And outside."

"A tree house?" Evan was practically vibrating with excitement.

"Uh…no." The risk of Evan being high above the ground was exactly the kind of thing Colin wanted to avoid. "But you'll like it. It will be big enough to invite friends inside if you meet some other superheroes in kindergarten. But in return for me building Super-Evan headquarters and my not telling your mom, you have to promise not to try to use any superpowers until you're at least six. No flying, and definitely *no* climbing on the stair rails, okay? Nothing like that. Deal?"

Evan stuck around for the two seconds it took to shake Colin's hand and retrieve his blanket, then he went running to find Henry and tell him all about the proposed headquarters.

It had been Colin's idea to put on a pot of coffee, but he wondered if Henry would notice if he didn't actually drink any. He felt keyed up already, jittery with too many conflicting and unexpected emotions.

"Mommy!"

Hannah was back. He heard the murmur of her feminine voice, undercut with the gravelly rumble of Henry's. Evan was louder than the other two, but except for that first shriek of greeting, Colin couldn't make out the rest of his words. At first, Colin didn't move—he'd been taking the second alone to regain his composure. But then it occurred to him that he didn't want to run into Hannah at the back of the house, amid her son's cherished belongings and in view of her gold-framed wedding portrait. It felt like crossing a line better kept between them.

They ended up nearly colliding just past the staircase. Hannah's brow was furrowed, and he could practically see little question marks dancing over her head as if she were a comic strip character. How much had Evan told her? He was sure the boy had omitted any mention of his near swan dive, but what had he said about their chat afterward?

"Any success at the estate sale?" he asked, as if his roaming her house while she was gone were a completely normal circumstance.

Nodding, she bit her lip. "Possibly too much success. Now that I have some furniture and accessories in my price range, I've got a better idea of what the finished cabin will look like. I want to get started."

"That's good, right?"

"Well, there's the matter of where you're going to sleep once we begin renovations. If you're sticking around?" she asked tentatively. "Evan said something about a clubhouse?"

Hell. He probably shouldn't have said anything without getting the mom's approval first. "Maybe I spoke out of turn. I was thinking that, if it's okay with you, I could build him a playhouse before I go. Something in view of the garden, so he has a place to safely hang out while you're working?"

Her liquid hazel eyes were pools of gratitude. "That would be *wonderful*. We were in such a cramped space in Colorado Springs that I thought all this fresh, open air would be good for him. I still stand by that, but I think it's overwhelming, too. I'm constantly after him not to get too close to the pond or mess around in the rooms upstairs or go to the stables without supervision. It'll mean a lot to a boy with Evan's independent streak to have a place all his own. But I don't under…" Was she afraid that if she pressed her luck by asking too many questions he might change his mind?

"My brother's getting married in a little over a month," he said. "After that, I have another job lined up, but I can give you that long. If you still want it. Plumbing's not my thing, but I'm decent at carpentry and have helped reshingle a roof or two. I can take over a lot of the stuff with the animals, too, which should free up some of your time."

"A month," she breathed. Her face was radiant, making her look entirely too much like a lottery winner. "That's fantastic! Come on, I'll show you the upstairs rooms." As she jogged up the stairs, she added, "They're not much to look at yet, but you never know. A lot can happen in a month."

Chapter Six

It had never been Colin's intention to grow a beard. Taking the time to shave now was simply a delayed reaction, not evidence that he was stalling or anxious about going to the main house for Sunday brunch. When Hannah had told him the Reeds were coming and asked him to join, there'd been no good reason to refuse. It was true that Colin had been trying to spend as little time as possible in the house, but he'd better get used to it since he was moving in this afternoon.

The thought was jarring enough that the razor slipped in his hand, and he scowled at his reflection. Not "moving in," he corrected. That implied a measure of permanence. His stay would be temporary, like renting a room in a hotel. *Yeah, except you're not paying a landlord. She's paying you.*

As he was leaving the bunkhouse, his cell phone chimed. He glanced at the display screen and saw his sister's name. Pulling the door shut behind him, he stepped into the spring sunshine and answered. "Hello."

"About flipping time!"

"I'm fine, thanks. You?" Despite the sardonic greeting, he secretly loved Arden's feistiness. It gave him confidence that she'd never take any crap from anyone.

And he took a certain selfish comfort in her strength. It helped reassure him that he hadn't screwed up too badly raising her.

"Seriously, do you know how many times I've tried to get in touch with you?" she continued as if he hadn't spoken. "You're like the worst brother in the world."

"Don't I get any credit for trying to call you two nights ago?"

Her *ffff* noise seemed like the verbal equivalent of rolling her eyes. "I can't believe the one time you bother phoning, I didn't hear it ring. Hope's cutting her first teeth, and she's not happy about it. The volume level gets intense."

"You sound awfully perky about a shrieking baby."

"I am!" Her voice was full of maternal pride. "The pediatrician is surprised she's teething this soon. He said he wouldn't have expected it for at least another month. Considering the complications during her birth, I was expecting some developmental delays, but she's been right on track for everything, even occasionally ahead of schedule. Garrett and I are really blessed. In fact…we're expecting another baby."

He took a deep breath, offering up a prayer for her safety and the unborn child's. "Congratulations."

As she chatted about the pregnancy, he got closer to Hannah's, spotting the Reeds' car parked out front. They were staying to help with the bunkhouse today. The four adults were going to rip up the ugly "all-purpose" carpeting and paint the walls. Hannah had ordered the replacement carpet, which they'd put down later this week. Meanwhile, there was a trailer full of furniture waiting beneath the carport.

"Even though I'm barely to my second trimester, I

look about five months along," Arden was saying. "Apparently, when you have back-to-back babies, you start showing a lot sooner with the second one."

He heard a bark, then Scarlett raced toward him at a dead run. When she reached him, she sat in the grass, tail thumping, and cocked her head in canine hello. Her tongue lolled out of her mouth, drawing attention to her crooked underbite. She looked so ecstatic to see him she was damn near cute. He scratched behind the dog's ears, not surprised when Arden worked the conversation around to asking when she'd see him again.

"The wedding's at the end of next month," he pointed out. "That's not long."

"I have a great idea," she said as if he hadn't spoken. "Elisabeth's family is throwing a couples' shower for Elisabeth and Justin in two weeks. Nobody expects you to come to Cielo Peak for that, but what if Hope and I drive down to see you? We can go shopping for gifts together."

"Or I can mail them a card and a check."

She huffed in exasperation. "I know shopping's not your favorite thing in the world, but man up. Justin's worth a little effort. Besides, are you saying you wouldn't welcome a visit from your favorite sister? I'm pregnant," she reminded him. "You should humor me. I'm emotionally fragile."

He bit back a laugh. His little sister was about as fragile and delicate as a charging bull. "Admit it, the shopping's a ruse. You just want to harass me in person and meddle in my life."

"Says the man who once threatened to break Garrett's kneecaps if he hurt me," she said wryly.

That wasn't meddling; that was being a brother. "As long as he keeps you happy, he's in no danger from me."

"I've never been happier," she said softly. "I can't even imagine how that would be possible."

He could hear the truth of it in her voice, and it made him smile. "I'm glad. You deserve it. Look, I have to go, but Elisabeth and Justin have one of those wish lists, right?"

"A registry? Yeah."

"Email me the information, and I promise I'll send them something more personal than a check."

"All right. But start answering your phone more, or I will program my GPS for Bingham Pass."

He tried to appease her without actually making any promises he might not keep, then they said their goodbyes.

Now officially late, Colin took the newly reinforced porch steps two at a time, Scarlett at his heels. He let himself in, calling "Knock, knock" as he approached. The buttery smell of pancakes beckoned.

He walked into the kitchen, where Evan, Annette and her husband sat at the table. Hannah stood at the island, slicing squares of hash brown casserole.

Her welcoming smile brought out her dimples. "You made it." She did a double take, her hazel eyes avid. "And you shaved. You look... I've never seen you clean-shaven." Her gaze slid over him, warm and sweet.

Colin swallowed. "It seemed like time." Acutely aware of their audience, he turned back to the table, ignoring Annette's raised eyebrows and extending a hand to the man who sat at her side. "Colin Cade, nice to meet you."

"Todd Reed." The man had a good grip.

Hannah had mentioned Annette's husband was an accountant. From the guy's stout build, buzz-cut auburn hair and skin that looked ruddy from time in the sun, Colin wouldn't have necessarily pegged him as having a desk job. But Todd's clear gray eyes radiated sharp intelligence.

Colin turned from greeting the Reeds and bumped fists with the little boy. "Mornin', Super-Ev."

He grinned, his face sticky with syrup. "Mr. Colin, are we going to start building my house today?"

"Not yet. But I did sketch some ideas last night. We can look at them later."

Colin poured himself some coffee and refilled everyone else's mugs. As he and Hannah sat at the table, he apologized for his tardiness. "My sister called with big news as I was leaving the bunkhouse. She's pregnant. Again." He shook his head. "Their first one's not even six months old."

Across the table, Annette's expression crumpled. "Excuse me." Her chair let out a discordant squawk as it scraped across the linoleum.

Todd's gaze was troubled as he watched his wife hurry from the room. Hannah sighed heavily. Evan kept shoving bites of pancake into his mouth, oblivious.

Colin caught Hannah's eye, keeping his voice to a whisper. "I put my foot in my mouth, didn't I?"

She leaned so close that the rich, feminine scent of her shampoo blocked out the food smells. He briefly imagined closing his eyes and breathing her in, tangling his fingers through the silky jet strands of her hair.

She brought him back to the present with her murmured, "Pregnancy's a sore subject right now."

"Sorry." He glanced to Todd, including him in the apology. The man nodded stiffly in acknowledgment.

When Annette returned to the table, she was composed, once again her smiling self, but Colin was careful not to mention babies or pregnancy again for the rest of the meal. After breakfast, all four adults helped clear the table, but Hannah insisted she had to load the dishwasher by herself.

"I'm obsessive-compulsive about where everything goes," she admitted with a self-deprecating grin.

"How about Annette and I go to the bunkhouse and start pulling up the carpeting?" Todd volunteered. The way he excluded Colin made it sound as if he needed a moment alone with his wife.

Colin nodded. "Sounds good. My stuff is packed up to bring over here, and I put the minifridge out on the carport. Only thing left to move is the bed."

Once the Reeds exited the house, Hannah instructed her son to put some toys and books in his backpack to keep himself entertained on the carport while the adults were painting. With four of them helping, it shouldn't take too long.

Colin stepped closer so that he could be heard over the running water as Hannah rinsed dishes without Evan overhearing. "I'm sorry I upset Annette. Did she… lose a baby?"

Hannah shook her head. "They're trying to get pregnant. No luck yet. Annette was trying some medication that might help, but the drugs make her pretty emotional. She and Todd have an appointment with a specialist coming up to discuss options."

Turning off the faucet, she stared sightlessly out the window, her expression faraway and pensive. "When

I first found out I was carrying Evan, I was thrown by the timing. I mean, I was happy, but because of when it happened, I knew Michael wouldn't be with me when the baby was born. I really regretted that. But I see now what a gift it was. If I hadn't conceived before he left…"

"It's amazing how you do that." That first afternoon he'd been here, she'd commented on her diminutive height, speculating that it made others see her as weak. Hannah Shaw was one of the strongest people he'd ever met.

She turned toward him, her forehead puckered in confusion. "Do what?"

"Instead of sounding bitter about losing your husband, who died too young on the other side of the world, you count your blessings."

"Being bitter won't bring him back."

"Do you still miss him?" He regretted the question immediately. It was too personal, too intrusive. Inappropriate, somehow, when he was standing this close to her. "I— Forget I asked. I'll go see if Evan needs any help gathering toys and make sure he isn't trying to dismantle his whole train set and stuff it into his backpack."

Not until he rounded the corner did he realize it was the first time in two years that he'd deliberately sought out a kid's company. But, for the moment, hanging out with Evan seemed a lot less complicated than remaining in the sun-dappled kitchen alone with Hannah.

ALTHOUGH COLIN GENERALLY preferred walking to and from the bunkhouse, it was logical to take the truck since they were bringing paint supplies, tools and outdoor toys for Evan. The little boy asked if he could ride in the bed of the truck with Scarlett. Since it was for such a short distance on private property, Hannah indulged him but only after dire threats of what would happen if he didn't stay seated and an announcement that she'd drive extra slowly for safety's sake.

As the truck began crawling forward, she gave an embarrassed laugh. "You must think I'm being ridiculous. At this rate, snails will pass us."

"It's never ridiculous to want to protect your child," he said softly. In his head, he heard the bone-chilling crunch of metal and glass, but it was a phantom memory. He hadn't been there that day, yet he'd relived the incident hundreds of times in his nightmares. He forcibly suppressed those thoughts, changing the subject. "I wanted to ask you a favor. Well, two technically."

"After everything you're doing for me and Evan? Anything you want!" Red bloomed in her cheeks as she reconsidered her statement. "I mean… What, um, was the favor?"

The way she stumbled over her words might have been amusing if he weren't suddenly having difficulty marshaling his own thoughts. He worked to think of Hannah in a platonic, she's-my-employer-and-nothing-more light, but she was a beautiful woman. The rosy blush and obvious direction of her thoughts only magnified her appeal.

He cleared his throat. "My sister's emailing me information for a gift registry. I, uh, wanted to borrow your laptop to do some online shopping. And I was hoping to get your opinion. This isn't my area of expertise."

Her face softened. "Baby stuff, huh? I can't wait until Annette does announce she's expecting. Buying clothes for infants is so much fun. And, needless to say, she will have the most awesome baby shower menu ever."

"This is actually for a wedding shower."

"Your brother's? You mentioned he's getting married."

"Justin," he said. It felt unexpectedly important that she know his brother's name. The more pieces of herself she revealed, the pettier it seemed that Colin never shared even casual information. "Arden's my sister, the youngest. After my parents died, it felt like the three of us against the world."

She turned to look at him when he mentioned losing his parents, but didn't ask for specifics. "So Arden's pregnant and Justin's getting married?" They rolled up in front of the bunkhouse, and she shifted the truck into park. "A lot to celebrate."

He nodded as he opened the door. Was it selfish, hiding out here in Bingham Pass instead of being part of the celebrations? Or did it give them room to experience their joy fully, without worrying about being insensitive to the brother who'd lost his entire world in one split second? Arden in particular seemed incapable of being in a room with him without pity haunting her gaze; Natalie's death had been nearly as difficult for her as for Colin. The two women had grown up childhood best friends.

He didn't want to be a black cloud hovering over other people's happiness, a grim reminder of how fleeting that happiness could be.

Hannah opened the tailgate. Evan scampered out of the truck like a monkey, Scarlett right beside him. The boy went straight for Colin's motorcycle.

"Stop right there!" Hannah pulled an old coffee can out of the back of the truck. It was full of large, colorful pieces of chalk. She drew a thick blue line across the concrete of the carport. "You don't go past this, understand?" At his nod, she added, "And when we're all done here, maybe we'll go fishing since you and Henry never got around to that yesterday."

The boy brightened, letting out a gleeful whoop that startled a nearby grackle and some sparrows into the air. He sat down with the chalk and his bag of toys. Hannah and Colin began unloading the paint supplies.

Reaching for a bucket of rollers and brushes, she slid him a curious look. "So you don't have a laptop? It's hard to imagine someone without a computer these days."

"A lot of my stuff is in storage, back in Cielo Peak. I've been on, I guess you could say, sabbatical." He hefted a can of primer. "I can check email and everything on my phone, but I don't like shopping on the small screen. Damn fingers are too clumsy," he admitted.

She laughed. "I watched you do detailed work on the porch—you're not clumsy. Your hands are just really big." Her gaze dropped as she spoke, and her cheeks flushed with color again.

An answering heat rose within him. He was grateful when the side door opened and Hannah looked away.

Annette stuck her head out. "You two need a hand out there?"

Hannah tried unsuccessfully to muffle a giggle. "Um, no, we're covered as far as hands go."

Colin bit the inside of his cheek to keep from laughing.

Once Annette had disappeared back into the house, Hannah said, "If I didn't say so already, of course you're welcome to use the laptop."

"And you'll give me your opinion on the gift registry? I don't understand why people need half that stuff." He recalled Natalie rolling her eyes when he commented that gravy boats were misnamed; they looked more like genie lamps than any boat he'd ever seen. "You, on the other hand, know your way around a kitchen better than anyone, and you have a flair for domestic details. I can't believe how much you've improved the living room and kitchen in one week."

Her smile was glowing. "That's the best thing anyone's said to me in months. Some days, it feels like such an uphill battle that I..." She shook her head in a visible attempt to dismiss doubts.

Realizing he'd said and done things to contribute to that self-doubt made his stomach turn. "Only way to get uphill is one step at a time," he told her. Wanting to put the smile back on her face, he teased, "This morning, I had a moment where I caught myself thinking Scarlett was cute. If that mutant mutt can look adorable, *anything* is possible."

THE FRESH PAINT on the walls and absence of criminally ugly carpet gave Hannah hope. There was more work to do, but at least now the space more closely resembled a potential guest cottage than an abandoned cabin where teens would get murdered in a low-budget horror film. But the fumes were too intense to stand around admiring their work.

She shooed everyone outside to breathe the fresh air. "Thank you, guys, so much for your help this afternoon. And yours, too," she told her son. While the rest of them were speckled with dabs and splatters of paint, Evan was covered in dirt and multicolored chalk dust.

"You helped by being so good." He'd kept his boyish impatience to a minimum. Hannah could count on one hand the number of times he'd whined that the project was taking "forever and ever."

"So we can go fishing now?" he demanded.

"Sure."

Todd sighed. "Not us, unfortunately. I've got paperwork I need to get in order for a client meeting tomorrow. But hook a big one for me, okay, buddy?"

"Okay." Evan nodded confidently, in no doubt whatsoever about his fishing prowess.

Hannah grinned. Sometimes her son's innate belief in himself was nerve-racking because, in a four-year-old boy, that occasionally translated to thinking he was invincible. But mostly his conviction that things would turn out for the best was charming. Growing up with no dad and having moved away from his friends in their former apartment complex, he could have a very different outlook on life. She hoped she was leading by example, showing him that happy endings were within reach of anyone willing to work for them.

Evan hugged the Reeds goodbye. As they were driving off, he tugged on the hem of Colin's T-shirt. "Will you come fishing with us, Mr. Colin?"

Colin hesitated. Even if he was simply stalling until he decided how best to say no without hurting Evan's feelings, she was gratified he hadn't refused automatically. Colin's teasing comment earlier made it sound as if Scarlett was beginning to grow on him. Was the same true of her son? That would certainly make it easier for all of them to share a house.

A zing went through her at the thought of sleeping under the same roof as Colin. It wasn't the first time she'd had a physical reaction today. *Be honest, it didn't just start today.* What about the cake she'd almost let burn yesterday because she'd become entranced by the sight of Colin riding Viper? And she was starting to have Pavlovian responses to the sight of his weathered cowboy hat.

Between grief, long working hours and the demands of being a single mom, she'd had maybe ten dates since Evan was born—and one of those was counting a man who'd bought her a coffee after he bumped her and spilled her first one. With only one unoccupied table left in a crowded café, they'd sat together and chatted for fifteen minutes. There'd been one man in Colorado Springs whom she'd gone out with three times, but when he kissed her, she'd had no response. It left her feeling flat and empty inside, and she'd wondered if her libido had died with her husband.

The only man she'd gone out with since moving was Gideon. She'd agreed to dinner to learn more about ranching, but he'd spent two straight hours talking about himself. She didn't learn anything useful, although she did leave the restaurant with keen insight into how he'd won a high school football game and what he looked for in a woman.

Aside from an occasional flutter when a hot guy delivered a great line in a movie, it had been a long time since she'd experienced much sexual interest. Now she was torn between wishing it was anyone but Colin who'd triggered it and simply being grateful she could still feel something. The key was to stick to *feeling,* not acting. As someone who'd been on the receiving end of sexual harassment, she knew better than to lust after someone who worked for her. Given Colin's customary aloofness, he wouldn't welcome the attention any more than she had. But even if the attraction were mutual—her palms dampened at the thought—she had an impressionable young child in the bedroom across the hall from hers.

She'd become so absorbed in her own prurient daydreams that she nearly jumped when Colin's deep voice broke the silence.

"Not today," he told Evan. He sounded almost regretful. "I've got some shuffling to do to get settled in my new room at your place. And I need to get started on my supply list for Super-Ev HQ. Which reminds me…" He walked to his motorcycle and unzipped a large black bag, pulling out a sketch pad. A charcoal pencil fell to the concrete. After retrieving it, he tore a page out of the pad and handed it to her son. "What do you think?"

"This is gonna be my house? Look, Mommy!"

The sketch was impressive, but given the hero worship in Evan's eyes, Colin could have drawn a lean-to held up with a stick, and Evan would have been delighted. It gave her a twinge to see how much Evan looked up to the man who'd be leaving next month. She found herself thankful Colin wouldn't be joining them at the pond. Evan might start to get the wrong idea.

"Would you mind taking Scarlett to the house with you?" she asked Colin. "I don't want to chance her jumping in the pond. You would think she'd know better when the water's still so cold, but that didn't stop her on a sunny day two weeks ago."

The corner of his mouth lifted. "What, bathing a muddy dog isn't your idea of a good time?"

With the playful light in his aquamarine eyes and that half grin, he went from being ruggedly attractive to one of the sexiest men she'd ever seen. "I can think of better ways to spend an evening," she mumbled. *Get a grip. He was making a joke about a mud-covered dog, not flirting with you.*

Apparently, Evan wasn't the only one in danger of wrong ideas.

WORKING INSIDE WAS never going to be as exhilarating as being outside in the fresh air and sunlight, but Colin was proud of his progress while Hannah and Evan fished.

When Hannah had shown him the upstairs, she'd talked about the work she'd need to do to make the second story inhabitable for guests. There were two pairs of rooms, each sharing a small connecting bathroom. She couldn't afford to renovate and furnish four bedrooms at once. He'd cleared space for himself and emptied out the adjoining one to give her a fresh canvas to work with. She was hoping to pick the best pieces of furniture from the combined rooms to set up a guest suite. He'd reinforced some slats in a bed frame, fixed a door on an antique wardrobe and was making plans to refinish a cedar chest.

Still, three pieces of furniture in a room painted the ugliest green he'd ever seen was barely a dent in the work to be done. He didn't think he had the energy to do much more today. Not the emotional energy, anyway. Arranging furniture was stirring up a lot of memories. He remembered the day he and Natalie had moved into their house. It had taken them hours longer than it should have because they kept stopping to make out in the different rooms.

He scrubbed a hand over his face. What was the point in torturing himself with memories of times he'd never get back? He'd survived the past couple of years by squashing those memories into the farthest recesses of his mind, but now they were refusing to stay buried. They seemed to be plaguing him more with each passing day.

Impatient and starting to feel suffocated by his own thoughts, he headed out to the barn. Horses were perfect company. They kept you from being lonely, but they didn't ask questions or expect deep conversation. Repressing the urge to saddle spirited Viper for a breakneck gallop across the property, he instead selected Apples. He and Hannah tried to make sure all four horses stayed in the habit of carrying riders.

After his ride, he found enough at the stable to keep him busy until after eight. It was full dark outside, the moon obscured by clouds, and Hannah's house was a blaze of light on the black landscape. The effect should have been welcoming, but it was also uncomfortable, like having the sun shine too brightly in your eyes.

Scarlett bounded to meet him when he walked through the door, and a freshly scrubbed Evan was close behind. He was wearing green pajamas covered with comical alien faces and his hair was still wet from a bath, the curls just starting to spring up around his shining face.

"You missed dinner," Evan said.

Feeling the truth of that in his empty stomach, Colin went straight for the kitchen. "How was the fishing? Did you catch anything?"

Looking up from a box of recipe cards, Hannah shook her head. "Only fish we saw today were the minnows I pulled out of the bait trap. Can't imagine *what* scared the other ones away. Hmm, what do you think, Evan?"

The boy giggled at the unsubtle accusation. "Mommy says I hafta be more quiet. I like loud."

Behind him, Hannah rolled her eyes affectionately. "Believe me, we know. But it's bedtime now, so you'll have to put the loud on hold until tomorrow."

All his time playing outside must have really worn him out, because he didn't even protest. He nodded to Hannah, then unexpectedly threw his thin arms around Colin's denim-clad legs.

"Night-night, Mr. Colin."

The berry scent of kids' shampoo and the stifled yawn in Evan's sleepy voice hit him hard. It took him two tries before he managed, "Night, Super-Ev."

In spite of being hungry mere moments ago, Colin made a half-articulate comment about needing to clean up and fled. In the upstairs bathroom, he was guaranteed absolute privacy. And if his cheeks happened to get damp, he could tell himself it was only the spray of the shower.

THE THUNDEROUS GROAN of the upstairs pipes was alarming. Hannah prayed the noise was due to infrequent use and not impending doom. While she knew how to utilize bargain finds to make a place homey and Colin was way better at carpentry than she had any right to expect from a veterinarian-turned-ranch hand, plumbing and electrical work would require paid professionals. On the bright side, horrifying mental images of a flooded second story kept her too preoccupied to envision Colin in the shower. So…there was that.

But now it was time to focus on baking the desserts

Patricia Loomis would be coming to pick up tomorrow. She wanted a trio of tortes for a dinner party, plus a baby shower cake for her niece—technically, several small cakes decorated to look like nursery toys. Hannah stood in the center of her kitchen trying to remember where she'd put the three-dimensional "rubber ducky" pan. She'd purchased it for a special order months ago and hadn't used it since. Which probably meant it was up high.

With a sigh, she dragged a chair over to the kitchen counter so that she could begin inspecting the hard-to-see shelf space above the cabinets. But even standing on the chair didn't give her much of a vantage point. She used the chair to boost herself onto the cabinet itself. *There.* On the very end, naturally. She'd been able to utilize the extra storage space only with a ladder and Todd Reed's help. The cabinets ran longer than the counter itself, and the last thing she wanted was to dig the ladder out of the garage at night, so she stretched as—

Hands clamped around her hips. Just below her hips, actually, more in the vicinity of her butt. Heat flamed through her.

"What are you doing?" Colin demanded, his tone rough. "Sometimes I don't think you or Evan have any survival instincts at all."

That stung. She smacked at his hands. "And yet we've survived the last four years without your help just fine." She needed to remember that. Colin wasn't staying, and it would be a mistake to become overly dependent on him.

"Get down from there." He didn't phrase it as a question, but there was something softening the edge in his voice now. Worry? "Please."

She allowed him to take her hand and help her down, which briefly brought her into contact with his body. He was wearing a pair of checkered drawstring pants and a heather-gray T-shirt—dressed for bed. There was a sudden melting sensation in her midsection. Seeing him like this was a novel experience. Without his boots and jeans and ever-present hat, it was as though he'd been stripped of his customary armor. This was a more vulnerable, approachable Colin. Touchable. *No, he's not. You need to keep your distance.*

To be fair, *she* hadn't been the one cupping *his* ass a moment ago.

"I'm over six feet tall," he told her. "If you need something up there, for pity's sake, ask me."

"I need the ducky pan on the end."

His forehead creased in a disbelieving scowl. "You were risking life and limb for a 'ducky pan'?"

"Risking my life?" *Hello, hyperbole.* She eyed the four-foot drop from countertop to tile floor. "You sound like my son, who claims he's *starving to death* if dinner's the tiniest bit late. Or that anything over fifteen minutes is *forever.*" She drew out the whiny emphasis on the words, trying to cajole a smile.

But Colin just glared. "You hurt your ankle earlier this week, and you've been on your feet all day. I saw how you were favoring your leg earlier. Which means your balance is less steady than usual. Can you imagine how much more difficult it would be to get your B and B up and running with a broken arm? You have to be careful!"

There was too much pain in his voice for him to be talking about sprained ankles and duck cakes. Where was this lecture coming from?

"I'm careful," she promised. "I'm a single parent who grew up in foster care. You don't think I've lost sleep, worried that something would happen to me and Evan would be left without a family? That he'd be alone, like I was?"

His face grew shuttered. With seemingly no effort, he hopped up on the chair and reached the cake pan.

"Thank you." Once she had the pan in her hands, she explained, "This may seem silly to you, but it's a paying gig for me. I was hired to make a complicated shower cake. Speaking of showers! My laptop's on the coffee table in the living room. Feel free to look at your brother's registry or check email or anything else that's inconvenient on your phone. If you bring it in here, I can look over your shoulder while I'm mixing and baking."

What was he thinking behind those blue-green eyes? She would have been content to keep trying to read them, losing herself in them until she reached some kind of clarity, but he was already walking away.

"Maybe tomorrow. I'm beat."

For a man who was supposedly fatigued, he sure was moving fast. He slapped together a sandwich, poured a glass of milk and then retreated back up the stairs.

She was tired enough to be punchy, making jokes in her head about the stranger who'd shown up just long enough to help a short baker in distress, then disappeared as mysteriously as he came. "Who was that pajama'd man?" she asked Scarlett.

Eventually, though, Hannah put thoughts of Colin aside and lost herself in the controlled chaos of baking. If someone were to walk in while she was in the middle of a project—with splotches of batter on the countertop, utensils and mixing bowls piled in the sink and confec-

tioner's sugar clinging to every surface it could find—
they wouldn't see order. But it was the precision that
Hannah found soothing. The measurements, the motion
of perfectly cracking an egg, knowing the exact amount
of vanilla to pour for the flavor she wanted.

While cakes were baking, she cleaned the kitchen.
Then she streamed a movie on her laptop while waiting for them to cool. She'd mixed the appropriate colors
for frosting and wanted to get a foundation layer on the
baby shower cakes before going to bed. She'd do the
final decorating touches before Patricia picked everything up in the morning.

It was nearly midnight before Hannah knew it. She
groaned at the clock, knowing she was going to hate
herself when it was time to crawl out of bed in the morning. She let Scarlett out one last time and was brushing
her teeth when she heard noises. A muffled moan, or
cry? Was Evan ill or having a bad dream?

But it was a much deeper masculine voice that split
the night with a shout. *"Danny!"* Colin's raw pain re-
verberated through the house, and Hannah found herself hurrying up the stairs. She didn't know whether
he'd appreciate her waking him from the bad dream,
but even if she weren't worried that a second scream
would wake up Evan, she wouldn't have been able to
leave Colin alone. No one should be trapped in a nightmare that vivid. His anguished roar had given her chills.

As it turned out, though, she didn't need to wake
Colin. When she reached the doorway of his room, she
saw him sitting on the side of his bed, feet on the floor.
Moonlight spilled through the window, casting a silvery
glow across his dark hair and bare shoulders. He didn't
look up, but his body tensed at her presence.

She felt like an intruder, yet couldn't bring herself to walk away. "Do you want to talk about it?" she asked softly.

"God, no."

She floundered, about to ask him if he wanted a glass of water before stopping herself, feeling stupid. This was not her four-year-old. Her mission had been to wake Colin, and since that had already been accomplished, she should just go.

"Wait." His voice caught. He still wouldn't look at her. "Don't…don't leave."

After a moment's indecision, Hannah stepped into the room. The bed creaked as she sat on the mattress next to him. She settled her hand over top of his, wishing she could do more but hoping this was comfort enough. There had been plenty of nights after Evan was born when she would have settled for someone simply patting her on the shoulder or giving her hand a reassuring squeeze. It would have been more than enough to know she wasn't alone in the world, with a new baby who was depending on her and no parenting experience.

You are not alone. Though she didn't speak the words, she thought them so loud she hoped Colin felt them anyway.

They sat there like that, in silence, and, after a while, his body began to relax. She stole a glance at his profile and was relieved that his jaw was no longer clenched.

"I'm all right now," he said gruffly. "Thank you."

She nodded, almost adding "any time" before catching herself. With any luck, it wouldn't happen again. And not just for his peace of mind, either, but for hers.

Sitting in the dark of Colin's bedroom and holding his hand, she'd felt a crack inside her, felt herself opening to him in a way she hadn't experienced for a very long time. In a way that—if she weren't careful—would hurt like hell when he walked out of their lives in a few weeks.

Chapter Seven

When Hannah stumbled bleary-eyed from bed the next morning, Colin had already left the house. There was a note on the table about his checking the young cows and starting to work with them to get them halter trained. She had to admit, she was a little relieved not to face him yet. Even though there was a lot she didn't know about Colin, for a moment, they'd shared an almost intense intimacy. She was hoping the false sense of connection would dissipate before she encountered him again.

She woke Evan, who was always at his quietest and snuggliest for the first hour of the day. Since moving to the ranch, she'd taken advantage of his not being a morning person, letting him sleep in while she tackled some chores first thing. But summer was just around the corner, then kindergarten would start before she knew it. For both their sakes, she should slowly help him adjust to the idea of rising on a schedule.

At least today she had a trip to town to help motivate him. Henry and Kitty were taking him into town for errands followed by lunch at Evan's favorite pizza place. Hannah, always looking for ways to make Henry feel legitimately useful without overtaxing his strength, had asked him to pick up some supplies, including new salt and mineral blocks for the cows and alfalfa seed.

Before much longer, she'd need seeds to start planting beans and squash. In Colorado Springs, she'd grown some herbs and window box tomatoes in the summer. But she loved having a real garden now. She was learning all she could about what grew best during the different seasons, and when she was working in the soil, her mind often drifted to the menus she wanted to offer her guests. She'd also started trading the first of her fresh produce, like radishes, to Annette in exchange for eggs from the Reeds' farm. Soon, she'd also have lettuce and carrots to show for her hard work.

Hannah had her list and envelope of money ready to go when the Whites arrived. She was glad to see Kitty was driving, because Henry seemed strangely jittery.

"Too much coffee," Kitty said in a whisper. "He's determined never to fall asleep on Evan duty again."

Again? Hannah didn't get a chance to ask because Evan was so excited about getting to help like a big boy—and, of course, the pizza—that he practically dragged the Whites out of the house. Hannah had plenty of peace and quiet to finish decorating her cakes and catch up on some laundry.

It was nearly noon when Patricia arrived. She was visibly surprised by the improved front porch. "Why, I almost didn't recognize the place," she commented, sliding her sunglasses atop her head. She had the same blond hair as her son, but hers was shot through with distinguished silver. "Gideon mentioned you had some extra help." Her mouth thinned in disapproval. "I can't say I would have hired Mr. Cade, given his reputation, but if this porch is any indication, I can't fault his work ethic."

"His reputation?" Hannah asked as she escorted the other woman inside.

"Did he tell you about the last place he worked? Or how he left after having an affair with the owner's wife?"

"What? That can't be right."

Patricia stiffened, sucking in a breath. "Are you calling me a liar? We've purchased three horses from the ranch next to the McCoy place, where he worked. They told us all about him. He's had a string of jobs." She made this declaration with a sneer. To Patricia, anyone whose family hadn't lived on the same property for six generations was suspect. "He was hired to help the McCoys with calving, but ended up destroying their marriage and leaving them in the lurch."

It was next to impossible to believe he'd abandon an obligation. After all, he'd stayed on Hannah's ranch initially because of faulty steps and his sense of responsibility, fixing something that was neither his doing nor his problem.

"Well," Hannah said, "as infallible as secondhand gossip is, I think I'll judge Colin on what I've seen of him." He was polite to Henry but companionable, too, not talking down to him in a "here, let me get that for you, old man" kind of way. And he was building Evan a playhouse with scraps from her garage and additional materials he insisted on paying for himself, since the project was his idea. They'd argued for ten minutes before she backed down because her budget was strained already.

"You certainly do make some interesting choices about men," Patricia said with a glint in her eye.

With an inward sigh, Hannah admitted to herself that she'd likely alienated her best client. *On the bright side, once you start booking guests, you'll be too busy to fill all of Patricia's special-order demands anyway.* She'd called twice this week to change her mind about frosting colors for the shower cakes.

Hannah gave her a wide smile, eager to see her on her way. "Need any help getting your cakes to the car?"

It wasn't until Patricia was driving off that Hannah asked herself the obvious question. *Why* had she antagonized Patricia in Colin's defense? She filled a pot with water and placed it on the stove, mulling over the situation as she retrieved a box of assorted tea bags from the pantry. As drawn to Colin as she was, she had no idea what he'd done or hadn't done up until now. Before yesterday, she hadn't even known he had a sister. She didn't know what had happened to his parents. Or who Danny was.

Maybe a woman? Dani could be short for Danielle.

The front door banged open and Colin called into the house, "Whoever just left was driving like a maniac. She almost mowed me down."

"Don't worry, I think she fired me, so it's doubtful she'll be back," Hannah answered. Should she tell him the driving might not have been lunacy so much as purpose? Patricia seemed to dislike him strongly.

His boots clacked against the faux hardwood in the living room, then he appeared in the doorway, his expression pensive beneath the brim of his hat. "We need to talk."

Did he mean about what had happened last night? She clutched the box of tea tight enough to dent the cardboard. "I'm listening."

"You might need to think about selling your bull."

"Huh?" It took her mental gears a minute to make the shift, but even once she refocused on the topic at hand, she was confused. Bulls had to be replaced, on average, every five years to avoid defects in the herd caused by inbreeding, but she should still have another couple of years before she did that.

"Last week, he was warning off Henry and me, showing us his side, pawing the ground, tossing his head. Today, he tried to kick me. Luckily, I've got good reflexes. It's not unheard of for bulls to be a little ornery, but he could be a threat to your and Evan's safety." He said the words fiercely. It called to mind the other times he'd been not only anxious for her safety but seemingly *angry.* His reaction was always disproportionate to the supposed "danger."

Something had happened to someone he loved. More recently than his parents.

"Who's Danny?" The words blurted out with no premeditation, and the blood drained from his face.

He swallowed hard. "My son. Danny was my son. He…died in the same car accident that killed my wife."

Oh, God. Sorrow washed over her. She both understood yet simultaneously couldn't imagine what he'd endured. No wonder he had trouble embracing optimism. If anything ever happened to Evan…

"I am so sorry."

"I was working. I wasn't with them. It was about two years ago." The words were awkward and mechanical, as if he were simply spitting out facts because he didn't know what else to say.

"And you've been on the move ever since?" Patricia

had insinuated he couldn't keep a job. More likely, he'd been running from his pain.

"No, I stayed close to family. Arden was so torn up, I didn't feel right about leaving Cielo Peak. Then she got pregnant and I promised to stay until the baby was born. It reached a point when I couldn't take it anymore, though. People say it gets better with time, but being in our hometown… Anyway. Now I'm here."

Not for long. They both knew that. Would he be able to heal drifting from one place to the next, without a support system? The Reeds and the Whites were invaluable to her. Maybe if Colin stayed somewhere long enough, he'd—

But that wasn't for her to decide. Opening the Silver Linings B and B was her dream, *her* fresh start, not his.

The only sound in the tensely silent kitchen was bubbling. "Your water's boiling," he said.

"I was making tea to go with lunch." She turned the dial to shut off the stove burner, then stretched on tiptoe to reach a bottle at the back of a cabinet. *Forget the tea.* In a completely uncharacteristic move, she poured a shot of whiskey into a glass tumbler, then quirked an eyebrow at Colin.

He opened his mouth as if to refuse, but then nodded. She set a second glass on the counter and poured another shot.

"In memory of those no longer with us," she said.

He stepped forward to take his glass and clinked it against hers.

The whiskey seared a hot path straight to her middle. Her eyes watered. "Wow."

"Been here a week, and I've already driven you to

day-drinking." Colin set his emptied glass on the island. "That can't be a good sign."

She put the whiskey back in the cabinet. "I don't plan to make a habit of it, so you're off the hook." He seemed quick to take responsibility for things that weren't his fault. Did he blame himself for not being with his wife and child? "Are you hungry?" Food was a time-honored response to grief. She had the sudden urge to make him a giant pan of macaroni and cheese, but it would be a lot quicker to reheat some homemade ham and lentil soup.

"I guess I could eat."

"Colin? I won't pry, but if you ever want to talk… When Evan was born, I tried to put aside all the Michael stuff. I couldn't cope with that and deal with a newborn at the same time. When Annette and I became friends, it all came pouring out, and it was such a relief." It had been like facing a horrible fear and realizing it wasn't nearly as bad as she'd dreaded. She was able to answer Evan's questions about his daddy without bursting into tears, was able to remember good times fondly instead of trying to ignore them as if they'd never existed.

"I appreciate the offer." But he had no intention of taking her up on it, judging from his tone.

She changed the subject. "That woman who was here earlier? Patricia Loomis, Gideon's mother."

He made the same expression she would have made if she'd stepped in cow manure. It almost made her smile.

"Seems she knows the McCoys," she said neutrally. "Just as a heads-up, Patricia also knows everyone in Bingham Pass, so there's a chance she might mention a dumb rumor about you and Mrs. McCoy."

"Good thing I'm not staying in Bingham Pass, I

guess." He leaned against the counter, regarding her curiously. "You said 'dumb rumor.' You don't believe it?"

"Nope."

"Thank you for that. Even my own brother double-checked with me to make sure it wasn't true. You'd think the numbskull would know me better than that," he grumbled.

Conversation turned to cattle while she warmed the soup and chopped veggies for quick side salads. Colin said he'd take care of "worming" the cows before he left next month and again urged her to consider replacing the bull. They talked about the considerations she should make and questions she should ask when buying a bull.

She shook her head, feeling as if she should be taking notes. "And I thought buying a new car was complicated."

He helped her carry bowls of hot soup to the table and, as he always did, removed his hat when he sat at the table. They didn't talk much during lunch, but with eating to distract them, it wasn't an awkward silence. And they both needed to get to other chores. She planned to work in the garden, and he wanted to reinforce some pasture fence.

"If I have time, I'm going to get started on Evan's house this afternoon."

It was a bittersweet thought, now that she knew he should be building a playhouse for his own son. But she kept her tone upbeat. "He'll be thrilled. We're both really grateful for everything you're doing."

"You're paying me," he reminded her wryly. "Even if you weren't, I'd probably be willing to do the work in exchange for just the food." He rose from his chair, plopping his hat back on his head. "Thank you for lunch, Hannah. You're a good…"

"Cook?" she supplied when he trailed off, a bemused look on his face.

"Friend." He sounded mystified by the word, as if he couldn't remember the last time he'd made one. "You're a good friend."

IT WAS A GOOD thing Colin spent so much time doing manual labor, because he couldn't remember having ever eaten as well as he did at Hannah's. At least, not since his mom had died. His father's official cause of death was heart failure, but it had seemed to Colin and Justin that their dad had simply given up on life after losing the woman he loved. Colin could empathize, but his dad's unwillingness to fight harder had ticked him off. What about the three kids who'd needed him? Once Colin had run the household, most of their dinners had come from the microwave.

Tonight, Hannah had served homemade garlic bread and a lasagna she'd called the secret weapon in her "nutrition arsenal." While Evan had been washing his hands before dinner, Hannah bragged about the veggies she snuck in amid the layers of pasta and cheese. Now that the dinner dishes had been cleared, she was reading Evan a bedtime story while Colin sat at the kitchen table with her laptop, finally making time to look at Justin and Elisabeth's gift registry.

There were a few whimsical items on the list that made him wonder if they'd taken Kaylee, Elisabeth's adopted daughter, to the department store with them. It was weird to think of his younger brother, the formerly confessed commitment-phobe, as a father. But there was no question Justin had grown to love Kaylee and would be a great dad and husband.

Colin braced himself, waiting for the dark anger to rise, the bitter rage that he was no longer either. But it was getting easier to separate his loss from his genuine happiness for his brother. Justin and Arden deserved their hard-won happily-ever-afters. At times, Colin had felt he'd been the luckiest of the three of them because he'd had the most years with their parents, the most normal childhood.

"All right, so what are we thinking?" Hannah's cheerful voice came from behind him. "Guest towels? Standing mixer? Pillow shams?"

"You do know it's weird that you sound downright giddy about those things, right?" Did her enthusiasm stem from growing up in other people's houses, dreaming of the day she'd have a home of her own? The way she talked about decorating this place, it was as if she wanted every curtain panel and sofa cushion to be just right, to match a picture she'd been carrying in her head. Would the reality live up to her dreams?

That was the problem with hope; its flipside was disappointment.

She pulled up a chair next to him, and he saw she'd changed clothes after tucking Evan into bed. There was nothing revealing or inherently alluring about the polka-dotted flannel pants she wore or the pale pink sweatshirt. But he couldn't help noticing she was braless beneath the soft material. That discovery was more distracting than it should have been.

He abruptly lowered his gaze. "What the…" Her slippers had tails.

She wiggled her feet, showing off the cow slippers.

"Aren't they great? They were a going-away present from some neighbors in Colorado Springs. To wish me luck as a cattle baron." Her dimples appeared. "Well, baroness. Lucky for you, all baronesses are born with exquisite taste." She waved her hand as if giving a royal decree. "Scroll away."

They looked through several pages of items, none of which felt quite right to Colin. Arden's mini lecture had obviously hit home. It felt coldly impersonal to send his only brother bath mats or a lamp. Hannah offered a compromise that included gifts Elisabeth and Justin had requested while still doing something that showed more thought than simply clicking an on-screen item.

"You can do a play on picnics," she suggested. "They want eight of those china plates. Buy two of those and that pair of wineglasses." She pointed. "Then you can get the pretty throw blanket that was on the last page and put it all together in a basket. Rather, your sister can, if we have it shipped to her and she doesn't mind. Voilà—elegant living room picnic! A perfect date night when you can't find a sitter and need something romantic at home. In fact, hold on…"

She took the mouse from him and opened a new window, browsing outside the registry. A few minutes later, she'd found a trio of ornamental candles that coordinated with the stuff they'd already selected.

"Nice touch," he said. "You really do have a good eye for this."

"The registry made it easy. It showed us what colors they're using and what their tastes are."

Sure, it wasn't rocket science, but he'd always been terrible at shopping. He prioritized function over form. The females in his life hadn't always appreciated that.

"I bet you'd get along with Arden. She's a photographer, all about space and light and color. When Natalie and I got married, Arden was our unofficial interior decorator." He was surprised his wife's name slipped out so naturally. But it felt right. For the past fifteen minutes, they'd been discussing Elisabeth and Justin's upcoming marriage. Mentioning his own was a logical progression.

Tentative but feeling unexpectedly liberated, he elaborated. "Arden and Nat were best friends, practically their entire lives. Whenever the two of them got together on a project, it was best to just stay out of their way. I worried about dating Natalie at first, since she was Arden's friend and younger than me. But once she got it in her mind that we belonged together, she wasn't shy about pursuing me."

She'd been a real dynamo, not intimidated by obstacles or setbacks.

He turned to Hannah. "She would have liked you. You're both very determined women." Natalie had been stubborn in a brassy, unmistakable way. With Hannah's dimples and mouthwatering array of baked goods, she was less obviously mule-headed. One could misread her sweetness as mild-mannered, but that would be a superficial conclusion. Only a relentlessly tenacious woman could accomplish what she was attempting.

"I take that as the highest compliment," she said, sounding pleased.

"Good. That's how I meant it."

He returned his attention to the laptop. They looked at baskets, checking the dimensions to make sure all the proposed gift items would fit inside, and Colin found himself volunteering more information he hadn't expected. He spoke softly at first, as if they were in a library. Or a church. "The only room I ever had much hand in decorating was the nursery. Natalie and I did that together."

"How old was he?"

"Two. He'd be Evan's age now."

She reached atop the table and squeezed his hand, the way she had last night. He stared at their fingers, his so dark and rough against hers, until the worst of the ache eased.

"After the funeral," he continued, "when my siblings finally left and I was alone in the house, I thought that room would be the worst to face. So I didn't. I shut the door and never went in. In the end, it wasn't the nursery that drove me to putting the house up for sale. It was the double vanities in the master bathroom. I had my mirror and sink, Nat had hers. Every damn time I brushed my teeth or shaved, there was her side. Empty. She used to gargle mouthwash really loudly and in odd rhythms to make me laugh. And before we went out to dinner parties, she'd talk to me while she was curling her hair, usually trying to guess what woman my brother would bring as a date. All those stupid little rituals."

"Laundry day." Hannah gave him a sad smile. "Michael and I met at a Laundromat, so that's where he proposed. He hid the ring box under some dryer sheets so that I discovered it, then made a big production of asking me to marry him in front of everybody. When we got married, we didn't buy a washer and dryer. We kept the Laundromat as a silly ritual, and when he was overseas, going to do laundry made me feel closer to him. When I had Evan and moved into an apartment that came with a washer and dryer, I cried every time I did the laundry. Which, when you have a newborn, is a lot."

She took a deep breath. "Eventually, the tears stopped and I no longer think of Michael every time I pour a capful of detergent. But he is still part of me. You asked the other day if I still miss him. I do, but it's different than it was. Whenever Evan reaches a milestone, I hate that Michael couldn't be here to see it. The first day of kindergarten is going to flatten me. But doing something with this ranch, which was in his family for years, is a way to honor Michael. We always knew we'd end up here—he was supposed to inherit it from his great-uncle—but I didn't have the B and B idea until last year. Sometimes I feel like…if I don't pull it off, I'd be, I don't know, letting him down. And I realize that's completely irrational, so don't feel compelled to point it out."

"You're a hell of a woman, and you're raising a good kid. I'm sure Michael would be proud." But her words struck an unpleasant chord within him. Since he spent most of his time trying *not* to think about Natalie or Danny, he rarely considered what his wife would have wanted for him. She knew how hard he'd worked to become a vet, and she'd always been one to speak her mind. What would she say about his current lifestyle? About his giving up the life they'd shared with no real plan for building a new one?

Maybe she'd call him a coward. And maybe she'd be right.

Chapter Eight

The Thursday-afternoon sun hinted at a hot summer to come, and Hannah was glad she wore a hat to work in the garden—and not just because it protected her face. She also hoped the wide, floppy brim helped disguise the number of times she stared in Colin's direction. He was currently atop a ladder fifteen yards away, wearing a pair of jeans that looked custom-made by the devil, hammering shingles onto the roof of Evan's playhouse.

He seemed to enjoy building as much as he did working with the animals; it was difficult to tell given the distance and sound of tools, but she could have sworn he'd been whistling earlier. And he'd been like a big kid last night, brainstorming ideas with Evan. Her son wanted a trapdoor for the playhouse, which Colin had nixed. But he'd appeased the boy with the offer of a periscope.

"You'll be able to spy on everyone in the area. I helped my brother make one when he was little. I think I can make one for your headquarters." After dinner, he'd amended the sketch to reflect some minor tweaks to the original design.

It had been nearly a week since he'd moved in, and it wasn't uncommon to see his sketch pad around the house. He'd shown her not only the blueprint for Super-

Ev HQ but a great sketch of Viper that captured all of the gelding's better qualities and made her forget what a pain in the ass the horse could be.

"You're talented," she'd told Colin the other day.

"Mom used to say I got it from her. When Justin was in high school, he begged me to draw a picture of this one girl he liked so he could claim credit for it and increase his chances of her going out with him. I refused, but he still ended up taking her to junior prom the following year. Lord knows what elaborate stunt he pulled to impress her."

From the stories Colin told, Justin sounded unrepentantly outrageous; it was difficult to picture him as the brother of someone so serious. "Does Elisabeth know she's marrying a con man?" she'd asked. The more she heard about these people, the more she wanted to meet them.

"Reformed con man. And don't worry about Elisabeth. She knows how to handle my brother."

Undoubtedly, the woman Hannah should be worried about was *herself.* She was having far too many moments like these—replaying conversations with Colin in her head, letting her gaze stray to him. His smiles were coming more easily, and the anecdotes he shared with her about his family and his past no longer sounded as if he were prying them painfully from himself with a crowbar. But the more he opened up to her, the more appealing he was.

Opening up to friends is what people do, she reminded herself.

And getting too attached to a cowboy with one boot already out the door was what fools did.

If Hannah thought she might actually be ready for

another relationship, there were at least a dozen women in Bingham Pass who'd offered to set her up with cousins and grandsons and coworkers. It seemed statistically impossible that any of those potential dates had as much emotional baggage as a man who'd lost both of his parents, his wife and his child. That much despair was staggering.

Her gaze went to Evan, who was blowing bubbles and laughing as Scarlett chased and snapped at them, and she closed her eyes in a brief prayer for his continued safety and health.

Noticing her attention, Evan ran toward the garden fence. He'd picked radishes for her, but harvesting the peas was a bit more difficult. "Mommy, are you sure Mr. Colin doesn't need my help? I'm a good helper."

"Yes, you are. But do you remember our talk about staying back while anyone's on a ladder?"

His face twisted into a scowl. "Okay."

"Tell you what, I'm almost—" She was interrupted by her cell phone, which was trilling her ringtone for Annette. "Hold on, honey. Hello?"

"I may have a lead on a horse! For you, I mean. You need more for guests, right?"

"Um…yes? But, practically speaking, I need guests before they can do any riding."

"I know. Maybe this is lousy timing, but you're the person who's always talking about positive thinking and seizing opportunities. Do you know Darcy Arrendale? She and her husband are divorcing, and she's got an everything-must-go mentality. They have to split the money from selling Ringo, and she said she'd rather sell him cheap to a good home than get top dollar and turn the money over to her husband, who, I quote, 'would just spend it on his trampy mistress.' She's doing this pretty quietly, but I told her you might be interested in coming by to see the horse. Did I overstep?"

"No. It never hurts to look, and I appreciate your thinking of me."

"Oh, good, because she's hoping you can come by this afternoon if you're interested. Apparently, some of her girlfriends are taking her away for the weekend. I've got her number, and if you decide to go over there today, you can leave Evan with me."

After they hung up, Hannah went into the house so that she could take notes while talking to Darcy rather than conduct the conversation from the middle of her garden. She took Evan in with her and settled him at the table with a frozen strawberry bar.

Richard Arrendale was the most successful real estate agent in Bingham Pass. She didn't know him well enough to know if he went by Dick or if that was just the moniker his soon-to-be ex-wife favored. Darcy used it about twelve times in their short conversation. As they were getting off the phone, she said with a sigh, "I just hate the way these men think they can do whatever they want—not just Dick but the whole 'good old boy' lot of them. He plays poker with Gideon Loomis and the bank manager. Between you and me, I think the Loomises hurt your chances of getting a loan. They've made it clear they plan to make an offer as soon as you 'come to your senses.'"

Cold fury knotted in her stomach. "Well, they'd better get used to disappointment, because I'm not going anywhere." Except to Darcy's to meet Ringo.

Hannah sent Evan to wash his sticky hands and to

change into cleaner clothes for visiting Aunt Annette. Then she hurried out to discuss the situation with Colin.

When he saw her, he climbed down from the ladder. He lifted the hem of his T-shirt to wipe sweat from his cheek, and the glimpse of hard abs almost made her forget what she'd come out to tell him.

"What's up?"

"Annette called me with what might be a serendipitous opportunity—she knows someone wanting to sell a horse cheap. But the words 'too good to be true' also come to mind. How much would I be throwing off your schedule if I asked you to go look at the horse with me? I'd appreciate a more experienced eye before I make any decisions I might regret later."

"Well, I have to check with the boss lady," he drawled. "She's a real slave driver. I should probably clean up first."

"We have time. Darcy's not expecting us for an hour and a half. Annette ran into her in town, and Darcy's not finished with her errands. Plus, I didn't know how long it would take you to reach a good stopping point, and we need to drop off Evan."

"Sounds like a plan, but word of advice? Any time you go to see a horse for the first time, it's not a bad idea to arrive earlier than expected. Unscrupulous people have been known to drug troublesome horses prior to the appointment to make them appear more docile."

"That's awful! Why do people suck? Obviously, not all people," she clarified. But definitely Gideon Loomis and his parents. "Life is tough enough without us sabotaging each other."

He hit the brim of his hat, tipping it back on his head so he could get a better look at her. "You okay?"

"Yeah." She got a little moody around this time of year—and a *lot* moody when people tried to screw her over—but none of that was Colin's fault. "I need to get back in the house, make sure Evan hasn't tried to repaint the walls or help himself to any unauthorized cookies." It had occurred to her earlier that maybe she should bake a cake for this weekend—Evan would certainly enjoy decorating it with her—but she hadn't been able to work up much enthusiasm for making her own birthday cake.

Colin joined them in the house a few minutes later, while Hannah was trying to give her son an explanation for why people had to wear shoes from the same pair and shouldn't just mix and match at will. Evan had decided he wanted to wear one red rain boot and one sneaker. She suspected this was because he couldn't find the other sneaker and suggested they look harder.

"The ladder and power tools are all secure in the garage, and I'm headed up to grab a quick shower," Colin told her.

She nodded. "I'm going to hunt through Evan's room for a missing shoe. If I'm not back in half an hour, send a search party." Her son's room was overdue for some spring-cleaning. She'd become so focused on renovating guest areas that she occasionally overlooked the private living spaces.

It took her only a few minutes to locate the sneaker, but while she was waiting for Colin, she took the opportunity to direct her son in some rudimentary tidying. Evan put toy cars into a plastic bin while she shelved all the picture books she found on the floor. She was considering dusting his dresser and the shelves lining his walls when Colin appeared in the doorway, his face puckered into a worried frown.

"What is it?" she asked nervously. No good news in the history of the world had ever been delivered with that expression.

"Maybe nothing, but you'd better call a plumber to double-check. I noticed something on the way downstairs. You have a flashlight?"

Stomach sinking, she grabbed one and followed Colin to the stairs. Even with the staircase light on, the windowless space was dim. Using the beam of the flashlight, he showed her some dark spots along the wall.

"It's possible you have some water leakage back there, maybe a broken pipe fitting or something. If so, it's important to find out where and fix the problem before it gets any worse. Water damage…"

She didn't even want to imagine the possibility of flooding or how costly that would be to repair. "I don't suppose there's a way to find or fix the problem without putting holes in my wall?"

His answer was an apologetic wince.

"Dammit!"

"Mommy?" Evan's voice at the bottom of the steps was scandalized. "We're not supposed to say that word."

She resisted the urge to bang her skull against the wall—why weaken its structural integrity further? "You're right, honey. Mommy forgot. Thank you for the reminder."

Colin's hand was warm and reassuring on the nape of her neck. "If it helps, you can swear all you want after we drop him off. I promise not to tell on you."

"Thanks." She bit her lip. "I should call Darcy back and cancel our appointment. If I'm about to spend thousands on plumbing repairs, I have no business buying a horse, even one that's unbelievably discounted."

"Don't panic," Colin advised. "At least, not until we know more about the plumbing. And even if you don't buy the horse, the act of inspecting him and thinking about the questions you want to ask is good practice. Come on," he cajoled when she remained tense and silent. "What happened to looking at the bright side?"

"You mean looking at the world through rose-colored glasses?" she asked drily.

He sucked in a breath. "Forget I said that," he ordered. "I was an ass. Just because I have trouble maintaining a positive attitude doesn't mean you should lose yours. Promise?"

He sounded so sincerely distraught by the possibility that she nodded. "I promise."

"Good. Then let's go see a woman about a horse."

AFTER THEY WERE finished at Darcy Arrendale's, Hannah called Annette to let her know they were on the way to pick up Evan.

"You sure?" Annette said. "He just ate dinner with us, and he's welcome to stay the night. You know I keep a spare toothbrush for him, and he had Trainket when you dropped him off, so we've got the basics covered."

Letting Evan spend the night with the Reeds would leave Hannah alone in the house with Colin on a night when she was feeling particularly vulnerable. *Oh, hell no.* "Absolutely not. You and Todd have a two-hour drive in the morning. You don't need my child waking you up at three a.m. for a glass of water."

Tomorrow, the Reeds had a consultation appointment at one of the best fertility clinics in the region.

"Any luck with the horse?" Annette asked.

"Not sure," Hannah said. "Colin suggests I always ask for a short trial period and that anyone who really cares about the horse should agree to that, but Darcy wants to get this over and done with before Richard catches wind of it. She assured me she has the legal right to sell the horse without him approving the sale, but it feels shady. I learned a lot, though." Colin had given her lots of tips that she might not have considered.

He'd said that any time a potential buyer arrived to find the horse already saddled, it was a red flag. A seller might be trying to hide that the horse was difficult to handle. Colin said she should always watch a horse be groomed and saddled. And while she obviously wouldn't buy one she hadn't ridden, he'd stipulated that she shouldn't ride a horse without the owner doing so first.

"Besides," she added, "none of the plumbers I called can come out until Monday. If I get good news, I can call Darcy next week and see if the horse is still for sale." Ringo was sweet. At ten years old, he might not have as many prime years in him as a younger horse, but he had experience. Colin said that horses with some mileage—assuming they'd been appropriately trained and well cared for—were much better with beginning riders. Most of her guests would probably not be equestrian experts.

When they got to the Reed farm, Annette told her there were leftover enchiladas. "Help us finish off this food so I don't have leftovers in the refrigerator. Todd and I were planning to stay out of town tomorrow night, anyway, instead of making the return trip, and now he's talking about staying through the weekend, making a minivacation out of it."

Hannah thought that was smart. The stress over not getting pregnant was taking a toll on the couple. A few days away would do them a world of good.

Evan met them at the door, a wireless video game controller clutched in his hand. "Uncle Todd was going to teach me a racing game. I'm gonna ask Santa to bring me one for Christmas!"

Bringing video games would first require Santa to bring a video game console. Which may not be in Santa's budget. "Um...December's a long way away," she said noncommittally.

Next to her, Colin's blue eyes had brightened with interest. "Which racing game?" He followed Evan, and within moments, all three males in the den were excitedly discussing video games.

"Boys will be boys," Annette said with a laugh. "No matter their ages, huh?"

Both women were amused when it was Colin—not Evan—who asked if they had time for one quick football game, promising to set short quarters. Todd had put away the racing disc and was showing Colin some of his other favorites. Hannah sat in a recliner with her plate, while Annette cheered on her husband and Evan rooted for Colin. Todd didn't score once. Colin decimated him.

He hoisted Evan on his shoulders for an impromptu victory dance. "This is the part where they pour Gatorade on us," he told the boy.

"On cream-colored carpeting?" Annette asked in mock horror. "I don't think so."

Colin was still grinning as he and Hannah herded Evan to the car.

"I wouldn't have guessed you were so good at video games," she said, holding out her hand for the keys. Now that she wasn't making a bunch of phone calls, she didn't mind driving.

"Are you kidding? Justin and I used to play for *hours*." He tilted his head at her. "Why would you assume I was bad at them?"

"Oh, it wasn't that I thought you'd be bad at them. They just weren't part of the picture I'd painted of you in my head." Were her cheeks getting red? "Not that I spend a lot of time thinking about this. But you don't have a computer and you carry charcoal pencils and a sketch pad in your motorcycle bag. I guess I had this vision of you as kind of a...bohemian cowboy."

He snorted, but tried to school his features into a serious expression. "Yes, a bohemian cowboy with many deep and mysterious layers. And a competitive streak a mile wide."

From the backseat, Evan asked, "What's com-petive?"

"Competitive," Hannah corrected. "It means when someone likes to win."

After a moment's thought, Evan proclaimed, "*Everyone* likes to win."

"Yes, but some people can get overzealous about it," she said.

"I don't know that word, either."

"It means they want it really bad," Colin said. "Some people get bad attitudes. You know that word?"

"Ohhh, yes. Mommy tells me all about attitudes."

Hannah stifled a laugh.

"I try not to get a bad attitude about winning," Colin told the boy, "and just try very, very hard to make it happen. Like your mom, putting so much effort into the ranch. She's a real winner."

"I want to be like her when I grow up," Evan said.

"Yeah." Colin smiled in Hannah's direction. "So do I."

EVEN BEFORE HABITUAL nightmares had made him restless, Colin had been a light sleeper. When he was younger, a sense of responsibility for Justin and Arden—a fear of losing any more family—had jarred him from sleep whenever he heard a noise. It had eased somewhat after he married, when he'd been content with life and had Natalie pressed against his side, but after Danny was born, Colin had quickly resumed old habits.

He woke early Friday morning, before the sun had fully risen, to the sound of voices downstairs. Then he heard the front door open and close. He'd slept in a pair of boxer briefs and a T-shirt. Now he pulled on a pair of faded jeans, washed so many times they'd lost their denim texture and were threadbare at the knees.

When he got downstairs, he found Hannah sitting on the sofa, her knees tucked up beneath her. There were no lights on in the living room, but she appeared to be staring at something on the coffee table. He squinted in the gloom. Was that a muffin?

"Morning," he said, trying to gauge her mood.

She didn't look at him. "Sorry if we woke you. Annette came by to bring me a cupcake on her way out of town."

His vision had adjusted. He realized the cupcake had a candle sticking out of it, and there was writing on the brightly colored wrapper. He couldn't discern any of the words but he could guess what they said. "It's your birthday?"

"Yep."

He sat on the couch with her. "So your friend decided to wake you up by delivering a cupcake at six-thirty in the morning?"

"She knew I wouldn't be asleep." Hannah sighed, pressing her head against the back of the sofa as she turned to look at him. "This is my first birthday since moving to Bingham Pass, but she and I have talked about it. This is the day that's the hardest. That sounds so selfish. You'd think it would be Michael's birthday, or the anniversary of when he was killed. But the first year we were married, he forgot my birthday entirely."

Colin let out a low whistle. Since his sister had also been his wife's best friend, Arden had usually started bugging him about coordinating birthday plans months in advance. But he knew the hell Natalie would have given him if he'd ever overlooked it.

Hannah's lips curved in a wistful smile. "He felt so terrible that every year after, he went all out. I mean, it was crazy. His birthday presents to me were bigger than Christmas. He 'kidnapped' me one year and took me cross-country to see a play on Broadway. We were only in New York one night. I've always wanted to go back when I had more time to sightsee, but it was an amazing night."

She gave herself a shake. "Wow. Pity party, table for one. Sorry—I'm fine. Next week, Evan and I will probably go to Annette and Todd's for a belated birthday dinner. You're welcome to come if you want."

"I may take you up on that invitation, but we're not waiting until next week to celebrate your birthday."

"Colin, seriously, it's okay, I just—"

"Is there a miniature golf course in Bingham Pass?"

Her eyebrows rose and she took a second to answer. "Not in town, exactly, but just on the other side of it. Annette and I took Evan once."

"Perfect." He draped his arm over the back of the couch, leaning in so she could see his resolve. She wasn't talking him out of this. Hannah took care of her son, went out of her way to make Henry feel useful, was building this ranch in part for her late husband and cooked for half the damn county. Today, she was going to let someone do something for her. "How about you meet me on the front porch at two o'clock? That gives me time to knock out some work, including your chores. You are under house arrest."

"But—"

"Take the day off," he said sternly. "Play with your kid, read a book, watch a dumb movie."

A smile lit her face. "And at two o'clock we're going to play minigolf?"

"Affirmative. Then we come back here, and I cook you dinner."

"That is incredibly—" She straightened. "Wait, didn't you tell me you were a lousy cook who microwaved everything you ever made for Arden and Justin?"

"And burned half of it," he said. "The other half was usually still cold in the middle."

"I suddenly remembered I'm on a diet."

He grinned. "Don't worry, Hazel, I got this."

"Hazel?"

"Oh." Before, he'd called her that only in his head. He hadn't intended to say it out loud. "Your eyes. You have beautiful eyes." He tried to say it matter-of-factly, but his voice was too low. Raspy.

Now it was her turn to respond with, "Oh."

Were they really sitting so closely he could feel her breath fan across his cheek, or was that his imagination?

"Colin?"

It was hardly the first time she'd said his name, but this time it did something to him. His body tightened, and he found himself angling even closer. "Yeah?"

"You have nice eyes, too."

One move of his hand—that was all it would take. If he lifted the hand at his side and cupped her face, would she meet him halfway? His gut said she would. And then he'd be kissing her.

He shot to his feet. "Two o'clock then?"

She nodded, her words shuddery and slightly out of breath. "Two o'clock."

In a spectacularly stupid lack of self-control, he reached out anyway, from a safe standing distance, and brushed his hand over her cheek. Her skin was velvety soft, and her long hair teased his fingers. She trembled beneath his touch, and he abruptly dropped his hand.

Thank God they'd have Evan to chaperone them on their trip to play putt-putt golf. Otherwise, it might feel like a date. As out of practice as Colin was with dating, even he knew it was customary to end dates with a good-night kiss.

Chapter Nine

Holy crap. The sentiment wasn't particularly eloquent or mature, but it kept repeating in Hannah's head as she listened to Colin's booted steps descend the porch stairs.

That had been hot. All he'd done was touch her face, but it had left her entire body tingling. Her heart was pumping as if she'd just chugged an espresso, and parts of her body she hadn't heard from in years were suddenly checking in to wish her a happy birthday. And to offer suggestions on what she should wish for.

For a second, she'd thought he might kiss her. And even though she didn't technically know what kissing Colin would be like, female intuition told her it would be richer and sweeter and more decadent than the world's best devil's food cupcake. Hell, just the way he'd looked at her made her melt.

She reached for the lamp on the end table, switching it on as if seeing more clearly might help her think clearly. Over the past few days, there had been moments… Sometimes he'd smile at her in a way that made her think she wasn't the only one stealing appreciative glances. He'd been more playful. After his taciturn first few days here, he was becoming quick to shower her with compliments. At first, they'd been about her cooking, no more personal than flattery Henry or Todd might have given her. But last night he'd upped the ante. When he'd told Evan she was a winner, it had been tough to contain her sigh. She'd grinned the entire drive home. Then there was this morning.

You have beautiful eyes.

She hugged a throw pillow to her body. As recently as yesterday, she'd been cautioning herself that it would be foolish to care too much for Colin. But a woman would need a heart of stone to resist a man who treated her like this.

"Mommy?"

Hannah whipped her head around guiltily, the same way she'd felt when she accidentally used the D-word in front of Evan. "Hey, honey. You're up early." No wonder—people had been coming and going all morning. She held her hands out for a hug, and he padded toward her, dragging Trainket behind him.

He snuggled against her, and she thought a day of "house arrest" with her kiddo actually sounded pretty perfect.

Suddenly, he gasped, his voice full of wonder. "Mommy, where did the chocolate come from?"

She started to tease "cupcake fairy," but he might take her seriously. "Aunt Annette brought it over as a present because today is my birthday. I was waiting until you woke up so we could share it. Want half a cupcake for breakfast?"

He nodded, his eyes eager.

"I have a surprise for you. We're going to watch cartoons and play games all morning. And after lunch, we're going to play minigolf with Colin."

Evan leaped from the sofa with an ecstatic shriek.

He ran in place for a minute, pumping his arms in a celebratory dance. Then he stopped. "I have a surprise for you, Mommy." He zoomed out of the living room and down the hall.

He returned with a folded piece of yellow construction paper, presenting it proudly. Multicolored glitter on the front formed a shape that was heartlike, and the word *MOM* had been written painstakingly in the center.

Love surged through her, a giddy pressure in her chest. "What's this?"

"I made a card at Aunt Annette's house. She said it was a secret mission. We hid it in Trainket when you came to get me," he boasted. Inside, Annette had written the words *Happy Birthday* and *I love you* in pencil, and Evan had attempted to trace over them in crayons.

"It's fantastic—the best card ever!" And for a day she'd been subconsciously dreading, it was off to a pretty fantastic start.

It was good that none of the cows got in the way of the tractor, because, today, Colin might not have noticed. He was preoccupied with the thoughts racing through his head. When was the last time he'd celebrated a birthday—his or anyone else's?

He honestly couldn't remember.

Then you're long overdue. The voice in his head sounded like Natalie's. She'd loved parties and social events. One year, when she'd informed him that she was throwing him a birthday party, he'd said it wasn't necessary and she'd teased that he had no say in the matter, she'd just been looking for an excuse to get a bunch of their friends together. Their circle of friends had been other young, married couples, some with kids, some without. Being around them had become even more wrenching than enduring the pity-filled glances of his siblings. As politely as possible, Colin had cut them all out of his life.

Now he found himself thinking about some of those former acquaintances, wondering if Peter or Don might want to grab a beer while he was in town for Justin's wedding. Or had they written him off as a self-absorbed jerk, too wrapped up in his own misery to be civil?

He was struck with an unexpected pang of regret. There wasn't one damn thing he could have done to keep from losing Nat and Danny. But what about the other people he'd deliberately lost?

Even though he'd stayed busy with a string of jobs, he'd been living in suspended animation. It was time to engage. Taking Hannah and Evan to celebrate her birthday was a start.

And nearly kissing her? What was that?

Before Colin had left Cielo Peak, there had been some dark moments, rare shameful nights when he'd tried to numb his pain by losing himself in physical oblivion. He hadn't been with any women he actually knew and he hadn't brought any of them home to the bed he'd shared with Natalie. They'd been frantic, hollow nights. He couldn't recall if he'd kissed any of those women.

If he kissed Hannah, there'd be no forgetting it.

The temptation was so strong. He hadn't felt that pull in so freaking long. But Hannah was a nice woman.

Yesterday, she'd responded gently to all of Darcy's vitriol about her cheating husband and marriage being a trap she should have never willingly entered. Hannah had advised the woman not to close herself to the possibility of love. As they'd talked, it had become evident that Hannah hoped she herself might eventually remarry. It was easy to envision. As nurturing and generous-hearted as she was, a man would be lucky to call her his wife. And a man would be one lucky SOB to have her in his bed.

Someday, she would find a guy who could love her forever, who would give Evan little brothers or sisters. Colin was a temporary figure in her life, a man with a truckload of abandonment issues and survivor guilt who'd alienated most everyone he knew.

Hannah was special. He hoped she got everything she deserved—and she deserved far better than him.

FROM THE PASSENGER SEAT, Hannah peered through the windshield and bit her lip to keep from laughing. Or groaning.

"So, as it turns out, there's an inherent flaw with impulsive, last-minute birthday party plans," Colin admitted sheepishly.

"Not checking the weather forecast first?" she asked. It had started to drizzle before they even left the ranch, but now it was pouring. This might be an even heavier rain than the storm that had blown through the day they first met.

At least one person in the truck wasn't amused by the situation. "Does this mean we can't golf?" Evan's voice quivered with disappointment.

"Well, it would be difficult to knock a ball into a hole that's full of water," Hannah said. "It would float right back out."

"No worries, Super-Ev. Do you know what a plan B

is?" Colin rolled to a stop at a red light, then turned to flash the boy a reassuring smile. "When your first plan flops, you devise a backup. I promised your mom a fun afternoon, and we're not about to turn around now."

"That's good," Hannah whispered, "because the road behind us may be washed out."

He smirked at her. "Quiet, you. Evan, ever been bowling?"

She was surprised when he nodded eagerly because she couldn't remember having ever taken him to a bowling alley.

"Uncle Todd has a bowling video game."

She had a few choice words for Uncle Todd—this time last year, Evan hadn't even been aware of what video games were. Now they found their way into his daily conversations.

"Great," Colin said. "Imagine that but with real pins and balls."

The bowling alley was down the street from the hardware store, where Colin had been making regular trips. There weren't many cars in the parking lot on a rainy Friday afternoon. But the ones present had taken up the front row. The only empty spaces close to the building were reserved for handicapped parking. Hannah asked her son not to jump in every puddle between the truck and the front door, one of his favorite pastimes. It was a measure of his excitement for their outing that he didn't even pout.

As they all unbuckled, Hannah reminded him not to open his child-size, superhero umbrella in the backseat. "Wait until right before you step out of the truck, okay?" She also kept a regular umbrella under the front seat of the truck, but she and Colin would have to share it. The thought of standing that closely to him made her pulse flutter.

He got out first, taking the umbrella from her and quickly crossing to her side of the truck, sheltering her and Evan as they climbed down.

Colin had showered after working in the pasture all morning—downstairs, as all the upstairs bathrooms were off-limits until after the plumbing inspection on Monday. He didn't smell like anything more exotic than soap and deodorant and himself, yet she still had to fight the urge to huddle closer and inhale deeply. His simple masculinity was far more enticing than any overpowering, lab-created scent designed to attract women. If cologne companies could bottle him, they'd make millions.

Colin opened the door, and Evan scampered inside first, wrestling with his umbrella to get it closed.

"Here, honey. Need some help?" Hannah offered.

"I'll get us a lane," Colin said. "Should I ask for gutter bumpers?"

"Bumpers?" she echoed. It had been a long time since she'd been bowling. And she'd never been especially good at it. "I remember gutter balls."

He chuckled. "They have something they can lay down in the gutters so that the ball doesn't consistently end up there. To keep certain bowlers from getting too frustrated and not having any fun," he said with a pointed look at Evan.

After a moment's consideration, she shook her head. "Let's start without the bumpers." Nobody was perfect. The important part was to keep trying, and she thought that was a valuable lesson for her son. Then again, they were here to have fun, so if it looked as if he was becoming traumatized by the experience, she was willing to revisit her decision.

Evan turned out to be completely fascinated by the concept of a place where they took your shoes and made you wear different ones. While he wiggled his toes in a pair of brightly striped, ugly bowling shoes, Hannah searched for the smallest-size ball she could find him.

"I like that one!" Evan pointed at a neon orange ball with green swirls. It was fourteen pounds. She immediately had visions of taking her kid to the E.R. for a broken toe.

"Maybe when you get a little bigger. Here, try this one." It looked as if the lowest weight the alley stocked was six pounds.

Colin was already entering their names into the automated scoreboard system. "You want to go first?" he asked Evan. He typed in Super-Ev. "Lots of great athletes have nicknames. What should your mom's be?"

"Birthday Mommy!" His voice carried.

An elderly man two lanes over called to the manager, "Hey, Bert! You do that singing thing like waiters at restaurants? We got a birthday over here."

Bert grunted. "This look like a restaurant to you?"

"You got nachos and beer. Close enough." The man waved to Hannah. "Many happy returns."

Once Super-Ev, Birthday Mommy and Cowboy Colin were all displayed on the overhead monitor, Colin took Evan to the side, on the carpet instead of the slick floor, and demonstrated the pendulum motion used in bowling. Evan's first attempt on the lane was, unsurprisingly, a gutter ball, but his second one managed to bump the pin on the far left. It wobbled for a full thirty seconds, then finally fell. Evan let out an ear-splitting whoop of triumph. Hannah knocked down the six middle pins and knew she didn't have a prayer of picking up the split.

Apparently, Colin was as good at bowling as video football. He got a strike right away, followed by another on his second turn. "If I get three in a row," he told Evan, "that's called a turkey."

But his third turn yielded only a spare.

"Oh, what a shame!" Hannah said to her son. "He didn't get his goose."

Evan giggled. "Turkey, Mommy."

"No." She pointed at the computer monitor, feigning confusion. "*Birthday* Mommy, remember?"

She half feared Evan would get bored since he got only one turn for each of their two, but he was having a blast. The two of them made silly jokes and laughed at the cartoon "replays" that showed on the monitor after each of Colin's strikes. And Evan was mesmerized with watching the ball return. He regarded it with awe, as though it were a futuristic transporter device.

Music played through overhead speakers, and when a song came on that she hadn't heard in years, she ducked down, taking Evan's hand and spinning him in circles on the carpet.

Colin laughed. "You're up, Evan. Maybe I can cut in?"

Hannah assumed he was kidding. The man had once gone seventy-two hours without smiling. He'd acted as if her standing on her kitchen counter would lead to a full-body cast. He seemed to lack the requisite absurd streak needed for dancing to a 1980s hair-band ballad in a bowling alley populated with retirees. She let out a squeal of combined shock and delight when he grabbed her and dipped her dramatically.

Behind the counter, Bert applauded them.

After they finished and went to return their shoes, Bert offered them a second free game in honor of Hannah's birthday.

"Not like I've got a long line of people needing that lane," he said with a shrug.

"Can we stay, Mommy?"

"It's fine with me. We have plenty of time until dinner." She knew Colin had made a brief run to the store earlier, but he'd shooed her from the kitchen before he put the groceries away. In keeping with his plan-B philosophy, she thought to herself that if whatever he was cooking didn't turn out, there was always peanut butter and jelly.

In the second game, Colin finally got his three-in-a-row strikes and Hannah declared, "Huzzah, a chicken!"

"A turkey," Colin and Evan corrected in unison.

Before they left, Bert made Evan's day—possibly his year—by hoisting him atop the counter and letting him sing into the bowling alley microphone.

"Do you and your dad want to serenade your mom for her birthday?" Bert offered.

"Oh, he's not my dad. He just lives with us."

There were guffaws from the other gentlemen gathered around, and Hannah felt her face go crimson.

"He's a ranch hand," she stammered. "At the Silver Linings." Though technically true, her words felt like a lie. There was no denying that Colin Cade was far more to her than just a cowboy passing through.

WHEN THEY WALKED into the house, Colin handed her a brown paper bag. "This is for you. Go enjoy, and Evan can stay and be my sous chef."

Evan nodded. "I'll help make soup."

While Colin explained that he hadn't said "soup chef" and that *sous chef* meant second in charge, she pulled a bottle of raspberry-scented bubble bath from the bag. She grinned. "Just what I always wanted. How did you know?"

Filling the tub made her think about the pipes in the old place, but she squashed her concerns in order to enjoy Colin's thoughtful gesture. When you were a mom—especially a single mom—a few completely solitary minutes to relax without interruption were a rare gift. But she didn't stay in the bath long. She was propelled by curiosity and the desire to protect her kitchen. Colin might be unaware of how quickly her son could destroy a room.

Hannah turned on the blow-dryer. Drying her hair completely took forever, but at least this way she wouldn't be dripping on her shoulders through dinner. She twisted her still-damp hair into a knot and secured it with a clip. She put on a pair of flannel pajama pants and a comfy sweatshirt, then frowned at her reflection, momentarily wishing she'd picked something more flattering.

Evan had apparently been appointed lookout duty because he was sitting against the living room wall. As soon as he saw her, he scrambled to his feet. "She's done with the bath!" he shouted, preceding her into the kitchen.

Hannah laughed at the container on her counter that bore the diner's logo. There was a platter of fried chicken sitting on the kitchen table, and she admitted some relief that Colin and Evan hadn't tried making it from scratch. The potential mess from frying chicken was daunting.

Colin caught her eye. "I heated it in the oven all by myself. And Evan and I worked very hard on the salads."

The salads were plated so that each one had two cucumber slices as eyes and a smile of grape tomatoes. There were also little bowls of mixed berries topped with whipped cream. Judging by the sheer amount of whipped topping leaning like the Tower of Pisa, she had a pretty good idea who'd been allowed to work the spray can. The finishing touches were a loaf of bake-and-serve bread from the market and a bottle of chilled white wine—or, in Evan's case, a carafe of chocolate milk.

Tears pricked her eyes, but they were happy tears. "This all looks incredible. I doubt they dine this well in the best restaurants in Denver."

Colin pulled her chair out for her. Once she was seated, he folded a dish towel over his arm and presented the bottle of wine for her inspection. Extremely elegant, even though the towel was hot-pink and printed with éclairs, bonbons and petit fours. She took a mental snapshot, knowing she would want to cherish this moment for a long time to come.

They took their time over the meal. She was halfway through her second glass of wine when she chased Colin away from trying to load the dishwasher.

"I'm the only one who does that," she reminded him. "I have a system."

He grinned, his eyes twinkling at her. "Control freak."

"Everyone's got their quirks."

She hated for the day to end, but they'd all been up

earlier than normal. Evan was visibly drooping. After he put on his pajamas, she tucked him into bed, suspecting he was sound asleep before she even made her way down the hall.

Colin was sitting on the couch. It was where they'd started this unforgettable day, and her body tingled with desire, a sense memory of how he'd made her feel that morning.

He held a large manila envelope. "I have one last thing for you. Consider it my version of a birthday card, although mine doesn't have any cool glitter."

She sat next to him, her hand unsteady as she slid a sheet from his sketch pad out of the envelope. Her breath caught. "This is wonderful."

He'd drawn her ranch, although he'd taken creative liberties with the position of things. The playhouse he was building Evan was out front, and a dark, curly head was visible through one of its windows. In the distance, a group of people rode horses. Scarlett was curled up on the beautifully redone porch, and the main gates were shown much closer to the house than they were in reality. The sign above them read SILVER LININGS. She wanted to frame it and hang it above the fireplace. It was a visual reminder of what she wanted to accomplish, and it had never felt so within her reach as it did right now, as if his drawing predicted the future.

"Thank you." She set the picture on the end table, then wrapped him in a hug. Lord, he felt good. All hard planes and corded muscle.

He stiffened—not, she thought, in rejection but more in surprise. Even though Evan had fallen into the habit of hugging him every night before bed, gestures of affection still seemed to catch Colin off guard, as if he was relearning human contact. But then his arms came around her and he was returning the embrace whole-heartedly.

"Happy birthday, Hannah." He brushed a kiss near the corner of her mouth. It was a quick, friendly peck, completely causal—except for how there was nothing at all casual about his nearness, the way he murmured her name. "I hope your wishes come true, and you get everything you want."

"Do you?" Her voice was husky. She didn't sound like herself.

Which was fitting because what she planned to do wasn't like her, either. But this was her birthday. If she didn't take the chance, she knew she wouldn't be brave enough to do it tomorrow or the next day. He'd opened a door between them when he'd feathered his lips over her skin in that teasing whisper of a kiss.

She wanted more.

Keeping her eyes locked on his, she moved forward slowly. The combination of anticipation and anxiety was causing her heart to pound so loudly he could proba-bly hear it. She was glad they were sitting—with their height differences, if they'd been standing, there was no way she could have done this without active coopera-tion on his part. When his gaze dropped to her mouth, it was as if he was already touching her.

She fit her mouth to his, and liquid fire roared through her veins. His hand tangled in her hair, bring-ing her closer, and he nipped at her bottom lip. Their tongues met, tentatively at first, but inhibition com-busted into fervent need. They tasted each other, explor-ing eagerly, and her hands were running up and down his arms now, over the well-defined muscles beneath his sleeves. He was strong and sculpted and so deliciously male she wanted to bite into him.

As if a dam had broken and he couldn't decide where he wanted to kiss her the most, suddenly he was everywhere. He moved from her throat to her jawline to her ear, and she moaned beneath the sensual onslaught. Shoving the baggy sweatshirt so that it slid off her shoulder, he followed the slope of her neck all the way to the strap of her bra. The moments blurred together, indistinct, a shifting kaleidoscope of sensation. She didn't know if he'd tugged her into his lap or if she'd moved there in her escalating need to get closer. He was hot and hard beneath her, and she reflexively rocked her hips against him. He groaned into her mouth, his kiss wild. Encouraged by his response and the sharp pleasure drugging her system, she did it again.

He threw his head back against the couch. "Hannah." It was an oath and a plea and an apology. "We..."

Face burning, she scrambled off his lap.

"That got out of control fast." He shoved his hand through his hair, his breathing choppy. "You told me this morning that today is difficult for you. I don't want to add to that difficulty, be something you regret in the morning. I have a few regrets of my own, and I can't do that to you."

"R-right." She'd be more impressed with his gallantry if every nerve ending in her body wasn't throbbing with fierce sexual need.

"Hannah? I'm not saying I don't want you." His tone was rueful as his eyes cut downward, indicating the physical proof of his reaction to her.

She made the mistake of following his gaze, and her yearning intensified.

"But we can't." He ran the pad of his thumb across her still-tingling lower lip; she hadn't realized how sensitive she was there. Then he added two of the most tantalizing, maddening words she'd ever heard. "Not tonight."

Chapter Ten

By the weekend, Colin was experiencing the worst insomnia he'd had in months. Although, maybe *insomnia* wasn't the correct medical term for the punishing physical discomfort of being hard enough to drive nails. He lay awake at two in the morning on Sunday, listening to the rain fall against the roof and windows. It was a gentle patter, almost lulling, except that it made him think of Hannah—how she'd looked in that soaked blouse the first time he'd seen her, how close she'd pressed to him beneath their shared umbrella on her birthday.

Who was he kidding? It wasn't the rain making him think of Hannah. He hadn't *stopped* thinking of Hannah since he'd pushed her away on the couch two nights ago.

He still hadn't decided whether that had been a noble act or perverse selfishness. She'd started her birthday with red-rimmed eyes and memories of her husband, claiming her birthday was the day she missed him most. Deep in some primal, irrational place inside, Colin hadn't been willing to share her. Granted, her earlier melancholy had seemed thoroughly vanquished by the time she'd reached for him on the sofa, but still....

He was a hypocrite. Last year, he'd indulged in a handful of faceless encounters meant to make him forget, to blot out the loneliness for a fraction of an instant, but he'd balked at the slightest possibility of being that for her. He'd already acknowledged that he couldn't be a permanent fixture in her life, wasn't what she deserved, yet he was equally unwilling to be a one-night stand. What *did* he want to be to Hannah? Until he figured that out, he'd been doing his best to avoid her.

Which would probably be a more effective long-term plan if he weren't also living with her.

THE FINANCE-INDUCED terror Hannah felt as she signed the check for the plumber Monday was a nice change from the pent-up frustration that had gripped her all weekend. With Colin's assistance, the plumber had sawed through the drywall and located the source of the leak. Colin had promised to refashion that section of the wall as a removable panel so that if she ever needed to get to the pipes again, it would be a simpler process. Plus, they'd planned to repaint the dingy stairwell a fresh, gleaming white anyway, so that would minimize the cosmetic damage. For the time being, the plumber had used some rubber hose to fix her problem, staving off further damage. But he warned that the best way to ensure she didn't come home to costly flooding some-day was to replace the faulty pipe. He put in an order for parts and said he'd be in touch to schedule his re-turn his visit.

She was facedown on the kitchen table when the phone rang. Rising from her chair, she prayed the caller was Annette. Hannah desperately needed to vent about the plumbing crisis, her wildly unexpected birthday cel-ebration and the way Colin was suddenly as skittish as a spooked horse.

His attempts to avoid her were humiliatingly blatant. Was he afraid she'd pounce on him in some hormone-fueled frenzy? But on the bright side, he'd spent every spare second over the weekend working on Evan's playhouse, and it was finished. Her son was ecstatic and had been disappointed she wouldn't let him sleep out there last night.

"Hello?" She answered without bothering to check the number first. If it was an unwanted solicitor, he was about to get an earful.

"Hannah?" Henry's voice was thin and reedy. "I hate to be any trouble, but could you come get me in the truck?"

Her heart jumped in her chest. Because Colin had been assisting the plumber behind the wall, Henry had gone out to the pasture alone. "Oh, my God, Henry, are you all right?"

He took a deep breath, and the way it rattled through the phone had her racing for the truck keys. "No, I don't believe I am."

HANNAH WANTED TO pace the hospital waiting room, but it didn't set a good precedent for Evan, whom she was trying to keep still and out of the way. Plus, she thought signs of nervous energy on her part made Kitty more apprehensive.

It had been a crowded truck ride to the E.R. Colin had offered to take Henry to the hospital so that she could stay home with Evan. She'd snapped at him that she realized he was trying not to share any space with her but that he was a moron if she thought she was going to sit at home twiddling her thumbs after Henry had been hurt on her land. The bull had charged him, knocking him to the ground.

"He's always been touchy," Henry had said in the truck. "Gotta be careful not to set him off, and it's a good idea to have a stick with you. But lately he's turned plumb mean. He didn't give me any warning, just came out of nowhere."

Because none of them had wanted Kitty driving while she was worried, they'd stopped briefly on the way to the hospital, just long enough for her to hop in the truck. When they'd all five unloaded from the cab in the parking garage, it had made Hannah think of a clown car.

Colin had helped Henry into the hospital, but once the nurse had taken him back for examination, Colin turned to Hannah, his face ashen.

"I need air. This isn't me avoiding you, I swear." His jaw clenched. "I hate hospitals. I'll be outside. Text me when you hear something?"

It was twenty minutes later when they were allowed to go back and see him. Henry's official diagnosis was a sprained arm and bruised ribs. The doctor said he should heal fine but added sternly that Henry needed to take it easy.

"No ranch work," Kitty told her husband.

"Seconded!" Hannah agreed. It was an unpleasant revelation seeing him here, under the fluorescent lights, with his arm in a sling. She was so used to seeing him ambling across the yard as if he belonged there.

He grimaced. "This mean I'm out of a job?"

"You are welcome at the Silver Linings whenever you want to visit us—which I hope will be often. You're like family." Hannah squeezed his hand. "But I couldn't live with myself if something happened to you because you were trying to help me. You recover. Colin and I can pick up the slack."

Panic clawed at her. Colin was staying only a few more weeks—unless what had happened the other night drove him to leaving sooner. Whenever he departed, the end result was inevitable.

She would be alone with no help on the ranch, faulty pipes, a drastically reduced bank account and a bull with anger-management issues.

COLIN STRODE TOWARD the house Tuesday afternoon. It was late enough that Hannah and Evan had probably already finished lunch. He didn't want to get in Hannah's way if she was baking, but he was starving. Would she be in the kitchen? He missed watching her flit from the pantry to the sink to the stove, moving with an endearing blend of grace and precision. Like a really purposeful butterfly.

In fact, he'd missed a lot of things about her. Going a few days without any prolonged conversation with her had highlighted how much they'd been talking up until then and how much he enjoyed it. They'd discussed their days of course, comparing notes on the ranch and laying out steps for what needed to be done, but he'd fallen into the habit of confiding more personal things, too. About the hilariously irate texts Arden sent when he didn't answer his phone, about the mentor who'd influenced him to become a veterinarian, about his nightmares.

Since that first night in the house, he hadn't had any other bad dreams. Lately, the only dreams he could remember all featured Hannah.

He'd pushed her away in case she was more emotionally vulnerable than she'd realized, but it wasn't her birthday now. He quickened his pace, motivated by the thought of her in that sunny kitchen, her dimpled smile, the addictive vanilla scent that always clung to her even when she wasn't baking anything. Jogging up the steps, he hoped that the car out front belonged to a customer who would be leaving any minute with a basket of cookies or pie pan of savory quiche.

He drew up short at the sight of Hannah at her kitchen table, so close to the sandy-haired man sitting next to her that they might as well be sharing a chair. They were both staring at her laptop screen, but he knew from experience that it was possible to do that with more space between them. A week ago, it had been Colin sharing the computer with her as she made jokes about her cow slippers and helped him put together a gift basket for his brother.

"Oh, hey." Hannah glanced up, meeting his gaze. "I put away all the leftovers from lunch, but the containers are in the fridge if you want to heat something up. This is Malcolm Kilmartin."

The man glanced up long enough to nod and smile before reverting his attention to the computer.

"Kitty found him for me. Her bridge partner is his grandmother." Hannah's smile was dazzling. It was nice to see her mood had improved. With the exception of a couple of single-word responses to Evan, she'd been silent the entire drive back from the hospital yesterday. "Mal's a computer genius."

The man grinned at her. "*Genius* is a strong word. I just have some experience building websites."

"He's only been here an hour and you should see the ideas he's already come up with," Hannah enthused, doing a happy little shimmy in her chair. "I'll be able to advertise for guests in the bunkhouse and have a whole section on the site called Hannah's Homemade, where people who live locally can place baking and catering orders." She rolled her eyes. "With any luck, that will stop people like Gideon from coming to hand-deliver orders in the future."

Malcolm shrugged. "Hard to blame a guy for finding reasons to come see you."

Colin narrowed his eyes. Although he was glad the guy was helping Hannah, Colin found it difficult to like the other man. He liked him even less half an hour later when, as Hannah walked him to the door, Malcolm asked her if she might like to go with him to the town May Day festival on Saturday.

Colin's fingers tightened around the dish he was rinsing.

"Oh." Hannah sounded surprised by the invitation. "That's… Thank you. Evan and I were already planning to go with some friends. Please come say hi if you see us there."

They stepped out onto the front porch together, and Colin didn't hear the rest of what was said.

Kilmartin was the kind of man who made sense for Hannah. While Colin had been eating lunch—which wasn't the same as eavesdropping—he'd discovered that Malcolm worked part-time in an office IT department, spent the rest of his work week consulting with private clients and volunteered as a kids' basketball coach at the rec center in the neighboring town.

If Colin's sister had brought Malcolm to a family dinner back before she'd met her husband, Colin may have even approved. The man seemed easygoing and intelligent, with a sense of humor. Hannah should be with a good guy, and, so far, Malcolm seemed exactly that.

Yet for the rest of the afternoon, as Colin pounded new fence posts into the ground, he envisioned Malcolm's face every time he swung.

IN THEORY, ANNETTE and Hannah were chopping vegetables for a salad while the men fired up the grill Friday night. In reality, the vegetables sat untouched on the kitchen island while Hannah pulled the glass pitcher out of the freezer to refill her friend's salt-rimmed margarita glass. Ever since Henry's injury, Hannah had been experiencing a vengeful craving for steak. And Annette had been fretting because they still hadn't properly celebrated Hannah's birthday. So they'd planned a cookout for tonight.

When the Reeds arrived, the first order of business had been Evan giving them the grand tour of his HQ. Todd was so impressed he'd asked Colin to help him build a toolshed on his farm. After the adults became busy with dinner preparations, Evan remained holed up in the playhouse. The dog was with him, and he'd declared her his sidekick. Yesterday, she'd been his arch nemesis. Scarlett's response to both roles was largely the same—happily padding after Evan wherever he went and hoping he'd drop food at some point. Evan and Colin had been trying to teach her to "play dead" this week to give her a broader dramatic range.

"Here you go." Hannah poured the margarita, teasing, "But if you suck this one down as quickly as the last, you're cut off."

Annette laughed. "Don't blame me. I *had* to drink something frozen. The looks you and your cowboy were exchanging left me overheated."

"I don't know what you're talking about." She totally knew what Annette was talking about.

Something had shifted this week. Colin had stopped avoiding her, but he hadn't kissed her again, either. He'd resumed his previous schedule of eating lunch and dinner with her and Evan. It was as if he wanted things to go back to a prebirthday normal. Except, he kept watching her with barely banked heat and hunger. The atmosphere in the house felt like a storm building. She was waiting for the storm to break.

Last night, she'd passed him in the hall with a basket of laundry and her body had grazed his. He'd inhaled sharply, his desire for her palpable. It had occurred to her that *she* could act on the powerful attraction simmering between them, as she had when she'd kissed him last week. Hannah wasn't a passive person.

But she was a trained pastry chef.

Cooking was often about patience, letting flavors build and waiting for transformations to take place. One did not rush a soufflé. There was an Amish bread recipe that took ten days to make properly. People didn't prepare Baked Alaska because it was easy; they did so because it was worth the time and effort.

Besides, Colin had shared anecdotes about how Natalie had pursued him, how his sister, Natalie's co-conspirator, helped scheme ways to bring her brother and best friend together. Hannah thought Natalie sounded like a lovely person, and what had happened to her was tragic. But Hannah wasn't looking to repeat history. She wanted Colin because he was sexy and principled and talented and surprisingly funny behind that sometimes-guarded interior—not because there was anything about him that reminded her of Michael.

"I don't think the two of you kissing was a onetime thing," Annette said. "He looks at you like he could throw you down on the nearest horizontal surface at any minute."

Hannah had to admit, the unpredictability was exciting. "Between you and me, I think it helped that Malcolm was here the other day." Had Colin heard the man ask her to tomorrow's May Day festival? "Is it wrong that I like the idea of him being a little jealous? I should be more evolved than that."

"As long as it's 'a little jealous' and not 'possessive stalker,' I don't see the harm in it. When Todd took me to my tenth high school reunion, we ran into one of my old flames. Todd was perfectly polite to him, but I could tell he was battling the green-eyed monster." She grinned over the rim of her glass. "It was pretty hot, actually. And so is your cowboy."

She liked the sound of that—her cowboy. But he was careful not to belong to any person or place. In a couple of weeks, he'd be gone. He'd been very candid about having a job lined up that started after Justin's wedding. He'd made a commitment. She knew he took those seriously.

Slumping into her chair, she asked, "What am I going to do when he leaves?"

"You mean because Henry's hurt and you won't have either of them to help around here?"

"You know that's not what I meant."

Annette's expression was full of sympathy. "Maybe it would be best if the two of you stay away from horizontal surfaces between now and when he goes. Why torment yourself with a taste of something you can't have?"

"Because I think I'd rather have the memory than say goodbye to him without exploring this, without knowing how good we could be together."

She was in the prime of her life, and she hadn't had sex in over four years. It hadn't bothered her much before, because there hadn't been anyone important enough to her that she'd wanted to make love. Colin was important.

The question was, how important was she to him?

"So." Todd Reed flipped over one of the steaks on the flame. "You and Hannah?"

It was such an abrupt topic change from plans for a toolshed that Colin wondered if Todd was purposely trying to catch him off guard with the question. Stalling, Colin sipped his beer, but no simple answer came to him. "Not exactly. She's a hell of a woman, though."

Todd nodded. "If it helps, she likes you. Since she's moved here, there have been a few guys interested. Gideon, of course, but also one or two who aren't buttheads. Mostly, she's been so focused on Evan and this ranch she doesn't seem to notice." He gave Colin a level look. "You, she notices."

He flashed back to those hot kisses they'd exchanged the night of her birthday. Yeah, she noticed him. And it was mutual. All week, the tug between them had been growing stronger. At least, it had on his end. It was difficult to say what she'd been thinking since she'd snapped at him on Monday for avoiding her. He hadn't meant to hurt her feelings. He'd only needed some time and space. Now he had more of both than he knew what to do with.

"How did you and Annette meet?" he asked. He was glad to be rediscovering the art of conversation, of making friends, but he didn't want to stand there dissecting his relationship with Hannah.

"She was dating my cousin. I knew the second I saw her that I wanted to be with her, but obviously the situation was complicated. I couldn't make a move until after they broke up, and even then she thought it would be too awkward. She took some convincing." He smiled at the recollection. "The challenge of wooing her was some of the most fun I've ever had."

Colin paused to consider what wooing Hannah might entail. Making birthday plans for her had been enjoyable, but those plans had included Evan. The idea of doing something specifically for her, something intimate and romantic—

"Unfortunately," Todd continued, "Annette and I have been facing a lot of challenges lately."

"The baby thing?"

"I'm trying to support her in this, but it's starting to take over our lives. We both really want kids, but I feel like, personally, I could be happy with just her. She's enough for me. I guess she doesn't feel the same way."

As a brother with two younger siblings, Colin had dispensed tons of advice over the years. He was a little out of practice, but the stark gloom in Todd's voice motivated him to find the words.

"You may be misreading her. I know she would love to have a baby, but maybe that's not the only reason she's upset. What if she sees this as her fault, worries that she's the reason you won't get to be a father?" No one wanted to stand between the person they loved and their happiness. "Maybe deep down, she feels like you deserve better."

Todd's eyebrows shot up. "Then she'd be crazy. I can't think of anything better than finding the right person to love and knowing they love you back."

It seemed like such a simple, comforting concept. But life took agonizing twists and turns. Colin knew that love alone didn't guarantee happiness. Perhaps that was why he'd been holding back with Hannah. He knew he couldn't offer her any guarantees.

Then again, since no one else could honestly offer them, either, what good did it do to keep his distance?

Chapter Eleven

It was so late when the Reeds left on Friday night that it was technically Saturday. Hannah flopped back on the sofa with a yawn. She'd had a great time, but now she was bone-tired. Far too exhausted to make it to her bed. *Maybe I'll just crash here.*

She always enjoyed Todd and Annette's company, but they'd been a welcome buffer tonight against the tension between her and Colin. And the longer they stayed, the more she'd gradually relaxed and enjoyed herself. The margaritas hadn't hurt. Todd had declined to try them because he had to drive home, which had made Hannah sigh, thinking of all the empty space upstairs. Lord knew when she would be ready for paying guests.

"Sure you don't want to stay the night?" she'd offered. "I am the proud owner of shiny new pipes that cost a fortune. I feel like more people should be using the second-story bathrooms now."

After dinner, she'd put aside her plumbing woes. They'd played a couple of kid-friendly games with Evan. After he'd been tucked into bed, they'd switched to poker for pretzel sticks and other card games that included a lot of good-natured trash talk. When Hannah had gone to put everything back in the closet, Annette had caught sight of the Clue board game, which led to lots of funny quotes from the movie. Even though it was after ten by then, the women had talked the guys into watching the DVD. A wonderful evening—but since she'd rolled out of bed at 5:00 a.m. to bake and decorate cupcakes, she was now thoroughly fatigued.

"Hannah?"

The voice startled her, and she sprang into a sitting position to find Colin leaning against the wall watching her. Oh dear heaven, he was shirtless. His damp hair was slicked away from his face, and he wore a pair of his usual drawstring pajama pants.

She made a valiant effort to unstick her tongue from the roof of her mouth. "I thought you'd gone to bed."

"Not yet." He grinned lazily. "I went up to shower and put those 'shiny new pipes' to good use. When I came back down, I wasn't sure I should bother you. You looked as if you might be asleep."

"In another three seconds, I would've been." She yawned again, covering her face with her hand.

"Well, since you haven't conked out yet, I wanted to ask you a question. Will you go to the festival with me?"

The request took her by surprise. He'd barely said anything when she and the Reeds discussed the festival earlier tonight, deciding where and when they would meet tomorrow afternoon. It would be Hannah and Evan's first time at the annual event, and Annette had recommended her favorite vendors as well as the best spinning rides to make Evan squeal with glee and make Hannah want to throw up.

"Sure," she stammered, realizing it was taking her far too long to reply. She blamed the contours of his shirtless chest. "If you want to come with me and Evan, we—"

"I don't just want to go with you. I want to take you. As in, a date. Between a man and a woman. And, obviously, her adorable four-year-old son," he added ruefully. "I don't want you to think of this as a friend or employee tagging along. I wish I could pick you up, that I had something to drive other than my motorcycle. So I guess I'm asking if I can take you out *and* if I can borrow your truck."

"A date?" She knew he'd said lots of other words, too, but that one had jumped out at her.

With a nod, he moved toward her. "Yeah. The kind where I tell you that you look nice, then I win you a large, fuzzy stuffed animal at an overpriced game booth and kiss you at the end of the night."

"Yes." Her heart was slamming against her rib cage. "I'd like to go on a date with you."

He gave her a brilliant smile. Then he leaned down, and she forgot to breathe. Had he decided not to wait for that good-night kiss? Because she was very okay with that. He lifted her hand and pressed a kiss above her knuckles. "Good night, Hannah."

How was she going to wait until tomorrow? And how on earth was she supposed to sleep now?

VEGETABLE SOUP MIGHT never be Evan's favorite lunch, but Hannah wanted to make sure her son got something resembling vitamins in his system before he started filling up on funnel cake and cotton candy. While he dawdled over his lunch, Hannah went to change. She was donating three freshly baked cakes as prizes for the cakewalk and hadn't wanted to risk getting frosting or batter on her dark sundress. When she returned to the kitchen, Evan scowled at her.

"You're in a dress." He said it like an accusation. "Do I hafta wear fancy clothes?"

She laughed. "No, you're fine the way you are." He was in boots, jeans and a T-shirt with a cowboy character from one of his favorite animated movies. She fought the urge to self-consciously double-check her reflection. Was she too fancy for an outdoor, small-town festival? She'd put on a long black cotton dress printed with small yellow daisies, paired with a light-weight denim jacket and boots. *Are you really going to take fashion criticism from a four-year-old?*

So what if she'd taken some extra time to curl her hair before pulling it into a bouncy ponytail? It wasn't as though she'd applied full makeup, only mascara and cranberry-colored lip gloss. Besides, isn't this what women did on dates, expended a little effort on behalf of a guy they liked?

When it was time to go an hour later, she was gratified to see that Colin had dressed a bit nicer than usual, too. He was wearing his best pair of jeans—what did it say about her that she knew his collection of jeans by heart?—and a button-down blue shirt, rolled up to expose sun-bronzed forearms. He was helping her carefully situate the cake boxes in the truck when Evan gave a small cry of dismay.

"I forgot my hat, Mommy!"

She unlocked the door for him and he raced to his room, returning with a black felt cowboy hat Henry had given him when she and Evan first moved here.

Evan mashed it on his head as he got into the truck. "Now I'm like you, Colin!"

Hannah had noticed that, somewhere around her

birthday, Evan's new idol had stopped being "Mr. Colin." The boundaries were definitely shifting.

It was a beautiful day. They rolled down the windows and all three sang along to Hannah's CDs. She'd heard Colin whistle or hum as he worked, but this was the first time she'd really heard his singing voice.

She was impressed. "You're good."

"Mom used to insist I got her voice, like I got her talent for drawing, but we all knew she was kidding." He chuckled fondly. "That woman couldn't carry a tune in a bucket. When she belted out Christmas carols, the neighborhood dogs buried their heads in the snow."

Hannah laughed at that, wondering absently what stories Evan would someday tell about her. Hopefully, he'd be able to say that she'd taught him about perseverance and the value of positive thinking. She wanted Evan to believe in himself and have the courage to follow his dreams.

Since pretty much the entire town turned out for the May Day festival, parking was an ordeal. After dropping off the cakes at the designated delivery area, they circled back block by block until they found a lot with open space. Hannah half expected her son to complain about the long walk, but he was too spellbound by the sight of the giant inflatables and large rides temporarily dotting the familiar landscape. By far the biggest attraction was a looming Ferris wheel at the center of the festival.

Evan craned his head all the way back, looking up with wide eyes. "I am not going on that."

Hannah squeezed his shoulders in a sideways hug. "You wouldn't like it anyway—it doesn't go fast enough for you." She knew from their trip to Heritage Square that he was a speed demon. He loved amusement parks. The only obstacle to his joy was frustration that he wasn't tall enough to ride every attraction.

They stopped at a booth to purchase a thick roll of tickets for the rides and games.

"What first?" Colin asked.

As expected, Evan asked for rides, jumping up and down enthusiastically to make his point. But they had to cross a midway en route to the closest ride, and he got distracted by the noises and sights, sucked in by the barkers' calls to win prizes.

Colin gravitated toward a booth where players threw darts in an attempt to pop colorful balloons spread across a corkboard wall. "My kind of game," he said, grinning. "You're looking at a two-time Peak's Pints dart champion. Our local bar back home," he said in answer to Hannah's quizzical expression. He ruffled Evan's hair. "You want to try?"

Colin exchanged two tickets for three darts and was handing them to Evan when he froze, his gaze contrite. "Sorry," he said to Hannah. "Probably should have asked if it was all right before I gave your kid sharp projectiles."

She laughed. "You have my blessing."

"That's a relief." He nudged Evan with his elbow and said in a stage whisper, "After this, we'll try running with scissors."

"Why?" Evan asked, his tone perplexed.

"Not really," Colin said. "It was a joke."

"Oh. It wasn't very funny. Knock-knock jokes are better."

Evan picked up his first dart, and Colin knelt down, helping him aim. The boy didn't put enough force behind his first throw, and it didn't even make it halfway to the wall. He did better with his second try and, with some assistance from Colin, popped a lime-green balloon on his third, winning a plastic horse.

When Colin offered to win something for Hannah, she suggested they postpone that for later in the day so that they wouldn't be carrying it for hours on end. "The horse fits in my purse," she said. "A giant teddy bear won't."

They navigated through the boisterous crowd and finally made their way to one of those awful "spinny rides of dooms," as she called them. It looked like a giant egg that had been cut in half to allow for passengers. The three of them squeezed onto the bench seat with Evan in the middle, and the attendant secured the small metal gate meant to ensure their safety.

Evan wiggled his body, too excited to sit still. "This is gonna be great!"

Then the buzzer sounded and the whirling began, and Hannah had a brief thought about the things mothers endured for the happiness of their children. Although she had to admit that this particular ride wasn't bad. Oh, it went on forever and Evan was screeching the entire time and the crazed looping, dipping pattern was every bit as nausea-inducing as she remembered. But Colin had his arm around the back of the seat, his fingers sliding over the nape of her neck, and the sensations that caused were so enjoyable she almost gave in to Evan's demand of "Again! Again! Again!" when the ride ended.

Colin laughed. "Pace yourself. We're going to be here until the fireworks tonight, so maybe we should see what else they have that we want to spend our tickets on, okay? We can always come back…" Frowning, he glanced at his phone, then tucked it back in his pocket.

"Everything okay?" Hannah asked as they exited the gated ride area.

He nodded. "My sister. Again. She's a little hyper-committed to staying in touch."

"Sounds nice, speaking as someone who's never had any siblings, hyper or otherwise." Sometimes she felt bad for Evan, an only child with no dad. Was she enough family for him, all by herself? But she brushed away the maudlin thought.

Colin gave her a sheepish look. "Didn't mean to sound ungrateful for having a sister who cares about me so much. I love Arden. I'll call her back when I'm not surrounded by so much background noise."

They passed by a corral where kids were getting pony rides, and Colin offered to stop if Evan wanted to participate.

Evan shot them the kind of disgruntled look Hannah expected to see a lot during his teenage years, along with the single-word caption *lame*. "I don't want to ride tiny horses. I want to ride Viper! I know I'm not big enough to ride him by myself, but can you take me, Colin?"

"We'll see."

Hannah got a text from the Reeds that they were running late, so they killed some time in the funhouse. Evan enjoyed the crooked walkways and trick mirrors. His favorite was one that had a normal reflection from the center of the room, but the closer you got, the taller you appeared. He went back and forth, laughing at his dramatic growth spurt. When he got back to where she and Colin stood in the middle, he linked hands with each of them. Reflected back at her were a good-looking man, a little boy having the time of his life and a woman who was dangerously close to being happy. They looked too much like a family, like a dream too treacherous to pursue.

Seeing so clearly what she wished she could have—what she wished she could give her son—caused a lump in her throat. "Need some air," she told the guys before dashing outside. "Feeling a little claustrophobic in here."

According to loan officers, there was a high probability her plan to turn an old ranch house into a tourist destination would fail. But better to channel her time and energy into something that had a chance than to try to build a future with a man still recovering from his past. She planned to make the most of her time with Colin and would try to view it as a gift. But then she'd have to let him go.

A LIVE BAND played inside a large tent with tiny white lights strung all around. It had been Annette's suggestion to come in and enjoy the music since none of the adults wanted to brave any zooming, zigzagging rides after eating dinner. They still had another hour until the fireworks display.

Within minutes, they'd found a table, although Evan had to share a seat with his mom. They piled the tabletop with purchases, including the carved wooden eagle Hannah had bought Henry as a get-well present, and prizes. True to his word, Colin had won Hannah a giant stuffed animal. Now she just had to figure out the proper place in the house for a lime-green octopus that was roughly the same size as Evan.

Annette sighed happily. "Nice to get off my feet for a few minutes after covering every square inch of the festival." Yet she was tapping her toes with enough vigor to jostle the table, keeping time with the lively song, and there was a wistful quality to her expression as she watched the couples spinning across the portable dance floor.

Hannah nudged Todd with her shoulder. He gave her a quizzical look, but then comprehension dawned.

He leaned over and kissed his wife on the cheek. "Dance with me, gorgeous?"

When they came back, Annette's cheeks were flushed and her eyes were shining. "I don't know why we don't do that more," she told her husband.

"From now on, we'll make a point of it," he promised.

Annette smiled. "Your turn, Hannah! We can watch Evan if you and Colin want to—" She broke off, interrupting herself. "Do you dance, Colin?"

He responded slowly, as if he wasn't sure of the answer. "I used to, but it's been a long time."

"At the very least, we know you can dip me," Hannah said, thinking of the bowling alley.

He grinned. "Well, that's a start. I'm game if you are." Rising from his chair, he took her hand. His thumb brushed back and forth over the spot he'd kissed last night, and a tremor of anticipation went through her.

She clasped one hand in his and slid the other above his waist, and everything else faded to black. She doubted that her rhythm was right because she could barely hear the music over her own heartbeat. He may have even stepped on her toes, but she couldn't feel anything beyond his hand at the small of her back. She wished it was a slow dance, so that she had a reasonable excuse to press herself against him, even with friends and family watching, but she made the best of the situation. It wasn't difficult to find a bright side when Colin was holding her.

The song was over too quickly, and she tried not to feel despondent as she returned to their table.

"We've been talking," Annette said, "and the three of us want ice cream. What if Todd and I take Evan, and we'll meet the two of you for fireworks?"

Which would give Hannah and Colin at least half an hour alone. Annette really was the best friend ever.

"*Please,* Mommy! Can I have a cone with just one scoop?"

He'd already had plenty of junk food today, but she supposed she could make an exception since the May Day festival came only once a year. She tried very hard not to think about Easter baskets, trick-or-treat bags, Christmas stockings or any of the other year-round opportunities to get cavities.

She took an extra moment to give the illusion of deliberation, then nodded. Her friends were even thoughtful enough to take all the stuff with them, Todd carrying the octopus atop his shoulders as if it was a young child. But the Reeds were so busy shuffling everything that they didn't realize Todd's wallet had dropped. Luckily, Colin spotted it before he took Hannah for another spin around the dance floor.

"Be back in just a sec," he told her, hurrying after them.

She was watching him walk away—and enjoying the view—when someone tapped her on the shoulder. She turned, half expecting Malcolm Kilmartin. Though she'd told him to look for her at the fair, she hadn't seen him all day. She wasn't looking at him now, either. Instead, she found herself face-to-face with Gideon Loomis.

Her mouth twisted. What did he want? "Hello, Gideon." Every time she saw the man, he wore a different cowboy hat. Tonight's was a black Stetson with a studded band.

"You owe me a dance," he informed her.

"How do you figure?"

"I won a cake of yours today." He put his booted foot on the empty chair beside her and winked. "Since you're responsible for the calories, it's only fair you help me work some of them off. Preemptively, so to speak."

Why did all of the man's attempts at flirting make her want to smack him with a rolling pin? Even though she'd been planning to dance, now she wanted to escape the tent. "I'm pretty beat. Comes with trying to keep up with a four-year-old all day. So—"

He grabbed her hand and tugged. "Hannah, Hannah, Hannah. When are you going to learn?" He chortled. "Loomises don't take 'no' for an answer."

"Do they take painkillers?" Colin asked mildly. "Because you're going to need one if you put your hands on her again."

Yanking her hand free, Hannah stood, putting herself between the two men. She should probably be appalled by the indirect threat of violence, but mostly she was just glad Colin had returned. "I was explaining to Gideon that I'm getting tired and was thinking about going elsewhere."

"Sounds good to me," Colin agreed. He shot Gideon one last fulminating glare. "It's too crowded in here."

As they emerged into the cool night air, Hannah jabbed him in the ribs. "Not that I'm ungrateful for the timely interruption, but you cannot go around threatening to beat up anyone who annoys me."

He ducked his head. "You're right. But don't you think me popping him one on the nose would be more humane than letting you Taser him?"

She laughed. "Let's just agree to avoid Gideon when possible. Although, I'm sorry we left the tent."

"I'm not," he said cheerfully.

"No?" Maybe he hadn't enjoyed the physical proximity of their dance as much as she had. There was a depressing thought.

"I have something else I want to do with you." Mischief laced his tone. "Without Evan around."

"Um…what did you have in mind?"

"You'll see." He reached for her hand. "Come on, Hazel Eyes, this'll be fun."

Ten minutes later, they were handing their tickets to the attendant at the Ferris wheel. It was all lit up for the night, and the garish lights of the carnival were prettier than they should have been. When she climbed into the suspended bucket, it immediately rocked back and forth. The motion didn't bother her when they were at ground level. Once they were one hundred feet in the air, however, she had a slightly more nervous reaction to the swinging. Wind curled around them, and she clutched Colin's hand.

He grinned, tightening his hold on her. "Maybe I should have taken you into the haunted house. That could have been fun. But this," he said as they rotated to the very top and stopped there, "is perfect."

His playful smile dissolved into something more intent, and he cupped his hand around the nape of her neck. She met him halfway, clashing in a hot, open-mouthed kiss. They were as hungry for each other as lovers who'd been separated for months. Throughout the day, wanting him had been a kind of sweet, heavy ache inside her, but now it sharpened to piercing need. Her fingers were meshed in his hair, her chest pressed to his when the bucket lurched. She realized they were moving backward, but she couldn't bring herself to break away yet. He kissed her all the way down.

They finally broke apart, and if she hadn't been too breathless to speak, she might have invoked her son's festival motto. *Again, again, again!*

He took her hand and helped her to her feet, not bothering to let go once she stood. They walked hand in hand to where they were supposed to meet the Reeds, and Hannah gave him a sidelong smile. After that explosive kiss, though, the glittery flare of fireworks was going to be a little anticlimactic.

EVAN FELL ASLEEP in the backseat of the truck before they'd even left the parking lot. Smiling, Hannah studied him from the passenger seat. He looked so serene, it was hard to reconcile him with the noisy little boy who'd thrown a fit when he'd discovered he was an inch too short to ride something called The Toxic Blaster.

She'd helped him pull off his boots while Colin started the truck, and his hat hung crookedly from his head. "He can just sleep in his clothes tonight," she said. Then she scowled, rethinking her decision. "Although I guess I should probably wake him to brush his teeth after all that junk food, huh?"

"It's one night. And you did give him that piece of plaque-fighting gum during the fireworks show."

She laughed at his earnest tone, not sure a stick of gum qualified her for Mother of the Year. "Oh, well. I'll make him brush twice as long tomorrow."

When they got to the ranch, Colin volunteered, "I'll get him. You're the one with the house keys."

She pulled them out of her purse and unlocked the door, pausing to shoo Scarlett outside for the night while Colin carried Evan to his room. When she joined them a few minutes later, he'd tucked Evan beneath the blankets and was standing by his bed with a heart-rending expression on his face. She wasn't sure she'd ever seen joy and sadness comingled so poignantly.

Swallowing back a tide of emotion, she passed him to drop a kiss on Evan's forehead. Then she took Colin's hand. "I know it's been a long day," she whispered, "but is it too late for that second dance?"

He shook his head. "I'd like that."

Her purse was on the end table in the living room, and she pulled out her phone, scrolling through her playlist until she found something appropriate. The music wasn't very loud, but it was enough for barefoot dancing in her living room, illuminated only by the spill of light from a tabletop lamp. Now that they were free of an audience, she put one hand on his shoulder and fit her body to his. It was closer than they'd been all day, but it still wasn't enough. Heat thrummed through her as they swayed, the friction of his jeans erotic through the soft cotton of her skirt. He was tracing his fingers up and down the length of her spine in a slow, sensuous manner that would have been relaxing if it weren't so arousing. Electric shivers broke out over her skin.

She craved his kiss like a drug, but not even standing on her tiptoes would bridge the gap between them. "Colin." His name was somewhere between a plea and a reprimand. "You did promise me a kiss at the end of the date."

His lips quirked in a wicked half smile. "Are you sure you want this to be the end?"

Chapter Twelve

Hannah's face was covered in a fiery blush, but she was smiling at his bold question. He found it impossible to look away from her mouth. The memory of how she'd kissed him on the Ferris wheel had him hard all over again.

"I don't want this to be over," she admitted. "I want you."

He cleared this throat. "Then maybe we should move to another room. One with doors." Once he got her out of that dress, he might not notice if a marching band came through the room.

She nodded. "Upstairs?"

His self-control lasted only until they reached the hallway at the top of the stairs. He backed her against the wall, holding her hands on each side of her head, fingers laced together, and devoured her with kisses. When he nipped at her throat, she arched her neck to give him better access. He released her hands long enough to remove her jacket, which crumpled to the floor with a soft thud. Her dress was long, but loose enough to give her freedom of movement. She hooked a leg behind his thigh, and he was cradled against her. For a second, he lost himself in the mindless bliss, rocking his hips and loving the sexy whimper that escaped her.

They might have made love there against the wall if they hadn't bumped a framed picture, knocking it askew and bringing him to his senses. His bed was around the corner and presented fewer safety hazards. He could wait the extra few seconds to be inside her. Maybe.

He stripped off his shirt on the way. When they reached the side of his bed, he gave her ponytail a light tug. "Take this down?"

She humored him, removing the elastic band with nimble fingers, and her hair spilled over her shoulders, framing her face. God, she was beautiful. He felt for a zipper on the back of her dress, but there wasn't one. She gathered the material at the hem and worked it upward, revealing her curvy body one dizzying millimeter at a time. She wore a satiny black bra and panties. The deceptively simple lingerie was a lot like the woman— not fussy, but feminine and stunning.

He cupped her breasts, running his thumbs over the tight peaks. She trembled so violently he was afraid she might stumble.

She seemed embarrassed by the intensity of her reaction. "Sorry."

"Don't be." It was powerful, knowing how he affected her.

She gave him a slight smile. "It's been so long, I..."

The last thing he wanted to do right now was talk, yet he heard himself ask, "Has there been anyone? Since..." It would be less complicated if she said yes. Four-plus years of celibacy was a lot of pressure.

Yet when she shook her head, he felt a rush of fierce joy. He was irrationally glad she'd waited for him.

He sat on the mattress and reached for her hips, pulling her into his lap. Unfastening the front clasp of her bra, he peeled back the silky fabric. He'd dreamed about Hannah like this, but the reality of her was incomparable.

He trailed his fingers across her bare breasts, then kissed a path from her collarbone to one nipple, sucking hard. She writhed against him. They rolled over on the bed, Colin impatiently shedding his jeans with one hand. Earlier in the week, he'd given in to the impulse to buy condoms, then called himself a fool the entire drive back to the ranch. Now the small foil packets in the nightstand seemed like his most valuable possession.

But first he needed to know that she was ready. Kissing her greedily, he lowered one hand to the slick folds between her thighs. She arched off the bed as he stroked her, her soft cries urging him on. The feel of her, the sound of her, was addictive. She tightened her grip on his shoulders. Her body stiffened and she threw her head back, her expression rapturous.

He sheathed himself in the condom and slid inside her, momentarily overwhelmed by how damn good she felt. She tilted her hips, silently asking for more, which he happily gave. They moved together, faster, more urgently, until the pleasure blotted out everything else. His blood roared in his ears, and he heard his own hoarse shout as if from a distance. Then he collapsed against her, holding her tight as if she were the most precious thing in the world. The way he felt at that moment shook him to the core.

They held each other in silence, and he was more content than he could remember feeling in over a year. But eventually, he was going to need to say something. He rolled away from her, uncertain. Most of the words that came to mind were too trite to encompass what they'd shared.

He simultaneously wanted to gauge her reaction and give her space. If *he* was this dazed, what must she be experiencing? It had been longer for her since she'd been with anyone and, on the whole, women were more emotional than men. What if she—

"That was amazing!" She sat up, unself-conscious in her nudity, and beamed at him. "We should do that again sometime. I feel…" She gave him a quick hug. "Did I mention *amazing?*" Then she climbed out of the bed.

He was surprised by her agility. He felt so wrung out he could barely move. In disbelief, he watched her shimmy into her dress, not bothering with her bra. Her denim jacket was still out in the hall somewhere.

He propped himself up on one elbow. "Where are you going?"

"To bake."

"At this hour?" Shouldn't she be mellow and sleepy? "You seem pretty keyed up. A less secure guy might worry you didn't enjoy yourself enough."

She leaned over and kissed him soundly on the mouth. "Oh, I enjoyed myself. Twice! Good sex is just really invigorating, don't you think?"

"Uh-huh."

"What may look like manic energy to you is actually a huge compliment, I promise." She blew him a kiss, then she was gone.

He blinked at the empty space in the room where she'd been standing a moment ago. Well. That was unexpected. No emotional drama, no need to talk things through, not even any freaking cuddling. He was relieved, of course, thankful she'd kept things so simple and light. It would be best this way for both of them.

He turned on his side and punched his pillow, trying to get comfortable. She'd seemed so unbothered about leaving him mere minutes after making such an intimate connection. It was almost discouraging. Then again…at least he knew for future reference that they were on the same page. They could make love without his worrying that she had the wrong idea about his long-term plans.

Maybe she was right—there was always a bright side.

It took about ten minutes for reason to catch up with the endorphins. Hannah stood at the kitchen island, eyeing ingredients that she shouldn't have pulled out. Once she put something in the oven, she wouldn't be able to go to bed until it was finished baking, and she'd barely had any sleep last night. Since she'd spent most of her day at the fair, she had a lot to catch up on tomorrow. *You need rest.*

But she hadn't been able to help her euphoric reaction. After a release like that, she'd felt as if she could fly.

In the past, Michael had teased that "normal" people didn't get that energized after orgasms. The way she saw it, her reaction was like a runner's high. Except what she and Colin had done was way more fun than running.

Still, now that a little bit of time had passed, she acknowledged that the wiser course of action would be to go to bed. She packed the baking ingredients back into the pantry and took a shower. Although the warm water helped relax her some, her mind was still racing.

She carried her phone into the bedroom and texted Annette You awake? Almost instantly, the cell phone rang. Hannah grinned. "I'll take that as a yes."

"Everything okay?" Annette asked.

"Wonderful." She scooted down beneath the covers. "Maybe that's the problem—it's been such a nice day that, subconsciously, I don't want it to end."

"If you're too restless to sleep, I vote you go upstairs and ask that cowboy of yours to do something about it."

"Um." Heat prickled in her cheeks. "Funny you should say that."

"Are you *kidding* me? Wow. I told Todd the two of you looked awfully cozy during the fireworks display! How do we feel about it finally happening? Excited? Regretful?"

How could she regret something so perfect? "I haven't felt this alive in... Well, it's been a while." Satisfaction had given her a potent buzz. She felt womanly and desirable and centered. "But I'm really rusty at this. I may have handled the afterglow part badly. I thanked him, then ran off to make cookies. Is that weird?"

"Yes."

"Annette!"

"There was a hot naked guy in the bed, and you voluntarily left? I'm sorry, but that's weird."

Had Colin wanted her to stay? Or had he been glad she didn't stick around, crowding him? It was disconcerting, to have been so physically attuned to someone yet still be left guessing what was going on in his mind.

And perhaps that was the real reason she'd sprinted out of there. Was she afraid to find out what he'd been thinking? If he'd told her he thought it was a mistake, she would have been devastated.

"I've been single a long time," she reminded Annette. "I'm not sure I remember how to do this."

"Colin's coming over to help Todd tomorrow with that shed. Do you want me to ask my husband to subtly—"

"No!" Having Annette ask her husband to do some digging on what Colin had thought of the evening, then report back, was immature, if not downright cowardly. "I will muddle my way through this without turning it into a group project."

"Fair enough." Annette sounded disappointed. "Don't overthink it too much, okay? First times can be awkward. Next time…"

Would there be a next time?

Colin had come so far from the haunted outsider who had changed her tire, but would he retreat after what they'd done? In the wake of their first kiss, he'd barely spoken to her for two days. It was possible he'd once again revert to a withdrawn loner. *I won't let that happen.* He deserved joy and laughter and playfulness in his life.

That rainy Wednesday night when Colin had first come here, she'd told Annette it was destiny, a sign that her positive thinking was working and that she could make the ranch a success. Which was a very self-involved analysis of the situation. Maybe fate had brought him here not because *she* needed help, but because he did.

COLIN SLEPT SO deeply that waking up was disorienting. He had to think about where he was and what day it was. But his first clear thought, aided by the wafting scent of coffee, was *Hannah.* Today was Sunday, which meant a big sit-down breakfast. After what had happened last night, he didn't know if Evan's presence at the table would make facing Hannah more or less awkward.

There was only one way to find out, though.

After a brief shower, he joined the Shaws downstairs in the kitchen. Hannah glanced up from the waffle iron when she heard his footsteps. She immediately looked away but then, resolutely, met his gaze. He could almost hear her inner pep talk as she told herself she had no reason to be nervous.

Colin wished someone would give *him* a pep talk. He was nervous as hell.

Evan, however, suffered from no anxiety. "Morning!" His greeting was crunchy around a bite of bacon. "Can we ride Viper today, Colin?"

"Sorry, but I won't be here. I have ranch chores all morning, then I'm helping your uncle Todd with a project this afternoon."

"But—"

"Evan, stop talking with your mouth full," Hannah reprimanded, handing Colin a cup of coffee.

Before taking it, he ran his thumb over her wrist, needing some physical contact no matter how slight. "Thank you." He glanced around the kitchen, unable to resist teasing her. "I was expecting piles of cupcakes and brownies."

"I did pull everything out of the pantry." She twisted her lips in a self-mocking scowl. "But then I realized I was behaving like a nutcase, so I took a shower and went to bed. Sorry to be so…me."

He shook his head. "If there's one thing you don't *ever* need to apologize for, it's being you."

Her smile heated through him faster than the coffee, and, if Evan weren't sitting ten feet away, he'd be kissing her already.

The phone buzzing in his pocket helped break the mood, and he retrieved it, expecting Todd's call. But

Arden's number showed up on the screen, making Colin wince. He declined the call, knowing she'd leave a message.

Watching him, Hannah opened her mouth to speak, then closed it. Then opened it again.

"It was my sister."

She nodded. "I suspected as much. I just don't— You know what? None of my business." She handed him a plate with a fresh waffle on it. "Although, you did say yesterday you were planning to call her back."

Eventually, he would. Talking to Arden, however, was something that required mental preparation, like the Graduate Record Examination to get into vet school. There were trick questions and awkward fill-in-the-blanks where he struggled to find the words to convince her he was fine and she should stop worrying so much. Most of the time, that required a lot of prevarication on his part.

Truthfully, he *was* doing better now.

But if he told Arden that, she would want details, would want to dissect his life in Bingham Pass. Whatever was developing between him and Hannah was excruciatingly new and raw. He wasn't ready to discuss it with anyone, much less Natalie's best friend.

He and Hannah had shared something important. Keeping it between them, protected from the outside world and isolated in the moment—away from painful pasts or uncertain futures—felt like the only way to safeguard it so they could enjoy it a little longer.

After breakfast, Colin complimented Hannah lavishly on her cooking in place of other things he wanted to say but couldn't in front of her son. However, when he came back to the house to grab a quick lunch a few hours later, Evan was playing in his room.

Hannah looked up from the huge sheet cake she was frosting. "Headed to the Reeds' now?"

"In a minute. There's just one thing I need to do first." Gripping her shoulders, he bent down and kissed her. She melted against him, sighing into his mouth as he deepened the kiss. When he straightened, he said, "Your baking is the best I've ever had, but you are more delicious than anything that comes out of this kitchen."

"Flatterer." Pleasure glinted in her bright eyes, reminding him of the way she'd looked at him last night as they eagerly helped each other undress.

With effort, he reminded himself that Evan could interrupt at any moment and that Todd was waiting.

"I don't know exactly how long I'll be gone, but I should be ho—" A pang hit him. No matter how comfortable he was growing with Hannah and Evan, this wasn't his home. They weren't his family. "I should be back by dinner."

"Okay." Her voice carefully casual, she asked, "What about after dinner? Any special plans for tonight?"

The smile she gave him sent need roaring through him. His mouth went dry, and he had to swallow before answering. "I'm at your disposal. Just tell me what needs to be done."

"Oh, I don't know." She peered up through her lashes. "Last night, you did an excellent job figuring that out with no instruction from me. I'm confident you will again."

As he left the house, Colin spared a quick mental apology to Todd. There was only one thing Colin would be able to concentrate on today, and it was not building a shed that was structurally sound.

A THIN SLIVER of moonlight shone through the window, lighting where her fingers were laced with Colin's. They were both lying on their sides, with his arm around her. Hannah couldn't see his expression, but the teasing note in his voice made it easy to imagine.

"I should probably let you go so you can alphabetize your spice rack or spackle holes in a guest-room wall," he said.

Was he never going to let her live down that first night? They'd been together four times since then, and although sex with him still gave her an incredible rush, she'd never left again with such a frantically awkward goodbye.

"It's uncouth to mock a woman while she's naked," she said primly. "And for the record, my spice rack is already alphabetized."

That made him laugh, a rumble that went through his chest and vibrated against her back. "You're right, I shouldn't mock you," he said, not sounding the least bit sorry. But he made up for it by trailing his fingers through her hair. He toyed with the strands and massaged her neck until she was thoroughly relaxed and drowsy. It would be so easy to close her eyes and drift off for a little while.

It wasn't until she jerked herself awake with a sharp jolt that she realized she'd actually started to doze. She should be in her bed. What if Evan called out for her in the middle of the night, or even came looking for her? And heaven forbid she accidentally stay here until morning. It wasn't just a question of what her son would think, either. She didn't know how Colin would react if she spent the night in his arms. It would alter the pattern they'd developed, their unspoken agreement.

During the day, they went about their work separately and kept their relationship scrupulously platonic. But she lived for that moment when, once Evan was asleep, Colin held out his hand and silently led her up the stairs. She hadn't fully realized how much she'd begun looking forward to that until she'd come up yesterday morning to work on one of the guest rooms. The simple act of walking up the staircase had left her besieged with mental images of them together.

And now it was time to go back down those stairs, to reality. With a sigh, she pulled away from him.

He kissed her shoulder. "Leaving?"

She nodded, half wishing he'd try to talk her out of it, at least for a few more minutes. "I need to go." But it was getting more difficult every time she did it.

WHEN SHE HEARD the front door open downstairs Saturday afternoon, Hannah experienced a twinge of vanity, wishing she'd had time to clean up after the past two hours of painting an upstairs bedroom. She knew she had flecks of pale peach on her denim shorts and her arms. With the weather becoming increasingly warm, she was wearing a tank top. Her hair was piled on her head and haphazardly secured with an elastic band. It was not her most glamorous look.

Yet when she reached the bottom step, Colin grinned, looking every bit as pleased to see her as he did when she wore a dress and makeup.

"Just the lady I was looking for. I figured everyone would be in the kitchen." He cocked his head, taking in the quiet. "Did you and Evan eat lunch already?"

Passing by him, she shook her head, relishing her secret too much to share it yet. "Nope." She detoured to
the front door and let Scarlett outside to run around the
ranch. Hannah might have to bathe a muddy dog later,
but making sure the dog didn't interrupt them would
be worth it. "Hungry?"

"I could eat." Lowering his voice, he added, "But
mostly I just want to be in a room with you for a while."

In the kitchen, she poured herself some water while
Colin pulled meat and cheese out of the refrigerator.
She downed the water, then shared her news. "It'll just
be you and me for lunch today. Evan isn't here. Annette
borrowed him as her 'excuse to see an animated movie.'
They left for a matinee about fifteen minutes ago."

Colin had gone completely still. "We have the house
to ourselves?"

"For at least two hours." She felt as wickedly liberated as a teenager whose parents left her alone for the
weekend.

His lips curved in that slow grin she'd come to love
so much. "And you were going to let me waste part of
it with a sandwich?" He advanced on her, scooping her
into his arms. Laughter burbled through her, accompa-
nied by need.

When he reached the bottom of the stairs, she said
breathlessly, "My room's closer."

Moments later, he was laying her across her bed. But
he didn't immediately join her. Instead, he stood, staring so intently that she squirmed beneath the scrutiny.

"What? Paint smears on my face?"

"No. I'm taking a second to savor the reality. I think
about you down here sometimes, after you leave my
room. There's just one thing…" He slid his fingers
through her hair and carefully removed the elastic band,

spreading the dark waves in a cascade across her pillow. "Perfect."

"A sweaty woman in cutoffs and speckled with Apricot Sorbet?" She smirked. "I think you may be confused about the definition of perfection."

He pulled off his boots, then rolled onto the bed with her, smiling into her eyes. "If I am, it's only because you redefine the word every day."

His words were like wine, making her light-headed with their sweetness. She tilted her face toward his, expecting a kiss, but he was preoccupied with inching up her tank top. It occurred to her that, previously, Colin had seen her body only in the dark. Now midday sun streamed through her windows. She had mixed feelings about that, but she got distracted when his fingers began following the path of his gaze, circling her stomach, dipping over her navel, teasing the underside of her breasts.

Arousal shimmered through her, her body liquid with it. But why should he be the only one who got to explore? This was a new opportunity for her as well as him. She let him raise the tank top over her arms, but then caught his hands when he reached for her bra.

"Your turn." Her voice came out in a husky command. "Lose the shirt, cowboy."

He was quick to oblige. She swallowed at the strong shoulders and chiseled chest he bared. If the man wanted to know the definition of perfection, all he had to do was look in a mirror. *And I have free reign to touch him.* Giddy with sensual power, she pushed against him with both hands, guiding him onto his back. She straddled him, then went up on her knees to slide off her denim shorts and kick them free.

Colin watched, rapt, his desire for her etched on his face. His obvious appreciation emboldened her. Eyes locked on his, she slowly removed her bra. He groaned, pulling her down for a hot kiss. Working together, they unfastened and removed his jeans. With his hands on her hips, he started to navigate her back atop him, but she had other ideas. They had two hours, and she wanted to make them count. She leisurely kissed her way down his chest and over the taut plane of his abdomen until she reached his erection. His hips bucked, her name a strangled cry on his lips.

By the time she finally seated herself on him, he let her set the pace for only a few minutes before rolling them both over and driving into her with desperate longing. Sensation tingled from the tips of her toes to the top of her head, and her climax was so explosive she felt as if she'd been flung from her body.

Once her vision returned to normal and she was no longer seeing bright red starbursts, her usual post-orgasmic delirious energy flooded her. She sat, grinning down at the big, strong cowboy who looked completely poleaxed.

"Still want that sandwich?" she asked. She was starving.

"Forget the sandwich." His breathing was ragged. "What I really need is medical attention."

She chuckled. "Should I apologize?"

"Don't you dare." He cupped her face in his hands. "That was…"

"I know." She kissed him, her humor fading into something poignant and a little scary. This was uncharted territory for them. They'd had sex before, but it was more personal, here in her bedroom, in broad daylight.

If they ate lunch quickly, they might have time to share a shower, which would be another first. Unsure where her bra had landed, she simply shrugged into Colin's discarded shirt. It fell nearly to her knees.

"I will be back with food," she promised.

"You're an angel." He had his arm thrown over his forehead, and his eyes were closed. Would he be asleep when she returned? She had some creative ideas on how to wake him.

In the kitchen, she made two sandwiches and put them both on the same plate. She also poured two glasses of ice-cold water, then carefully balanced it all to carry.

Colin was wearing his boxer briefs but nothing else, and the sight of him sitting in her bed felt so natural that she wondered how she'd get used to his *not* being here. He reached for the plate and one of the glasses. She set the other on the nightstand, then moved away from him.

"You're not joining me?" he asked, puzzled.

"I'll be back in a flash." She'd decided that, as a precaution, she should text Annette with a request to call when they were on their way back. It would be easy for Hannah to lose track of time, and the last thing she wanted was to be caught unaware when her son came barreling into the house at his usual Mach 10. But her cell phone was in her purse on the living room coffee table.

She'd just scooped it up when she heard a vehicle outside. Her heart beat a staccato rhythm as she gauged the distance to the hallway. They hadn't bothered to shut the storm door, and she'd be visible through the screen. *Crap.* Unless the projector at the movie theater had malfunctioned, there was no way Annette was back so soon. Hannah wasn't expecting anyone else. Whoever it was, it looked as if she'd be chasing them off dressed only in Colin's shirt. Luckily, it more than covered her. She tried not to think about her disheveled hair.

A closing door was followed by quick footsteps on the porch. She craned her head around to peek and felt her jaw drop in surprise when she locked gazes with the stranger. He was shorter than Colin and there were crinkles around his eyes, a mobility to his face that made him look as if he laughed easily and frequently. But the handsome features and dark-haired, light-eyed coloring were the same. Although she'd never seen a picture of him, she knew instantly who he was.

"You're Colin's brother," she said through the screen.

He looked every bit as surprised as she was but recovered with a grin. "Yes, ma'am. I'm Justin—the good-looking Cade brother." There was no come-on in his tone, just a surfeit of humor. "And based on your knowing me, this must be the right place. Hannah Shaw?" His gaze swept over her, his eyes dancing. "It's a pleasure to meet you."

Chapter Thirteen

When Colin heard the familiar sound of his brother's voice, his first thought was that he must have fallen asleep while waiting for Hannah to return. *Having a nightmare.* He hadn't been able to stomach the idea of so much as talking to his siblings about Hannah and her son. Actually facing them here at Silver Linings would be infinitely worse.

But then he heard the murmur of Hannah saying something he couldn't make out and Justin's unmistakable laugh in reply. Dear Lord—it wasn't a dream. *What is he doing here?* As Colin shoved his legs into his jeans, he glanced around for his shirt, belatedly remembering that Hannah wore it. Was she wearing anything else? Jealousy pinched at him. Colin loathed the idea of any man seeing Hannah without all of her clothes, even knowing how devoted Justin was to his fiancée.

Then Colin realized that, for all he knew, Elisabeth had come along with his brother. It could be a damn family reunion right in Hannah's living room. A cold sweat broke out on his forehead and he lumbered toward the front of the house, uncharacteristically clumsy and feeling as if he were slogging his way through waist-deep wet cement.

Hannah flashed him a bemused smile over her shoulder. "Look who's here." She didn't seem to mind the intrusion, but he was sure she had questions about why Colin's brother had suddenly appeared out of the blue.

She's not the only one.

"Justin, have you eaten lunch?" she asked. Colin had long since recognized that offering food was her default setting when she wasn't sure how to handle a social situation.

"Yes, ma'am."

"Well, I insist you stay and join us for dinner," she said, pointedly ignoring Colin's scowl. "I don't know what your plans are, but you're welcome to spend the night, too, if you're not picky about the digs. We're in the middle of redecorating. Colin can show you upstairs. Meanwhile, I'll go..." She glanced down as if just remembering her unorthodox wardrobe. Her gaze slid to Colin's bare chest, and her cheeks flooded red. They might as well have been wearing sandwich boards that read We Had Sex. "I'll, um, let you two catch up."

She made tracks for the back of the house, where her bedroom door shut loudly.

Justin's eyebrows shot up, and Colin silently dared him to say anything about their appearances. But for a change, the Cade who had a quip for every occasion was at a loss for words. So Colin started.

"What the devil are you doing here?"

"A guy can't come visit his big brother?"

Narrowing his eyes, Colin waited for the real answer.

"Could be worse, bro. I could've brought Arden with me."

Colin barely repressed a shudder.

"Hey, if you don't want our sister sending out search parties, you have to learn to answer your phone. She's got a bee in her bonnet. With my wedding fast approaching, she's worried that you…" He looked uncomfortable.

It took a second for Colin to follow the implication. With Justin about to tie the knot, Arden was concerned about the poor widower in the family, afraid the wedding would bring up too many difficult memories for him. Truthfully, her own ceremony *had* been tough for him. But now—

Guilt nailed him with the force of a ricocheting bullet. He realized he hadn't thought about Natalie or Danny a single time in *days.* It was as if they hadn't even existed. What was happening to him? When had he made the shift from enjoying an affair that he and Hannah both recognized couldn't last to playing house with her and Evan?

Justin was talking again, faster now, as if he could patch the gaping awkwardness with words. "Anyway. You know how Arden is. And it's worse with her pregnant. She almost jumped in the car and tracked you down herself, but Garrett talked her out of it. Our compromise was that I'd take the weekend off and come check on you."

Justin's primary job was ski patrol, but during spring and summer months, he worked at the lodge his future in-laws owned, leading hikes and rafting excursions and administering first aid. "I'm sorry I haven't been taking her calls," Colin said gruffly. *Very* sorry, now that he was paying the consequences. "But I needed time alone, space to think." *In other words, get lost.* "Good news, you don't have to sacrifice your weekend babysitting me. Go back and tell our sister I'm…fine." He choked on the word. Ironically, he had been doing fine.

But the sudden realization of just how well he'd been doing knocked him for a loop. It was if he'd fallen into an alternate reality.

"Go back? I just got here." An unrepentant half grin tugged at the corner of his mouth as he met Colin's irritated gaze. "Besides, the lady of the house invited me to stay for dinner."

HANNAH REALLY LIKED Colin's brother—Justin Cade was funny and charming and quick to offer his help, both with painting upstairs and peeling potatoes for dinner. Yet as enjoyable as his company was, she kind of wished he'd go away and never come back. Because ever since he'd shown up at her front door, Colin had withdrawn so far that he was a shell of himself.

Dinner was bearable only because Justin and Evan carried the conversation. Her son had been delighted by their surprise guest, and Annette had been so openly curious that Hannah had been afraid she'd have to set an extra place for supper. But she'd finally managed to shove her friend out the door, knowing Annette would be phoning later with questions. *Maybe I just won't answer.*

Then again, from what she'd gleaned, Colin was the recipient of this brotherly visit because his siblings had reached their limit with him not taking their calls. She found the evidence of their concern endearing. Judging by Colin's dark scowls, he did not share this opinion.

Hoping that good old-fashioned comfort food could help defuse the tension that had been building all afternoon, she'd fixed meat loaf, mashed potatoes and some green beans that Annette had canned last year. Justin's eyes had lit with pleasure at the first bite, but Colin was hardly touching his food.

Colin was also not making eye contact with her. He'd kept his distance ever since Justin's arrival. They'd always tried to keep their relationship discreet, but his current behavior leaned more toward outright shunning her. She tried not to be ticked off, knowing he hadn't expected this, but his distance stung. It was as if he were ashamed. No matter how much he avoided speaking to her or touching her, it was too late to hide the facts from his brother. There was no way Justin hadn't already drawn the correct conclusions after finding them half-dressed and tousled in the middle of the afternoon.

If Justin had been shocked to find his widowed brother cavorting with his new boss, he'd handled it with aplomb. But finding out she had a child was a different story. He'd been openly troubled when Annette dropped off Evan, staring from her son to Colin, surprise warring with apprehension on his handsome features. Whatever worries he had about Colin getting involved with a single mom, he'd pushed them aside to entertain Evan with stories of his own childhood.

Most of the stories were about scrapes Justin had gotten into and Colin's attempts at creative punishment. "He's so much *old*er than me," Justin stressed teasingly over a dessert of butterscotch pudding, "that it was almost like he was my dad."

Evan nodded, easily relating to Justin's growing up without a father. "My dad's dead, too." His fleeting moment of seriousness evaporated into boyish curiosity. "So what did Colin do to you when he found out about the car?"

As they cleared dishes from the table, Justin made an effort to include Hannah in the discussion, too. "By the way, thank you for the gift basket. Elisabeth and I both loved it."

She was startled by the unexpected gratitude. "That was from your brother."

"Who, when left to his own devices, usually sticks a check in the most unimaginative card he can find?" Justin guffawed. "I don't think so." Lowering his voice, he reached out to squeeze her shoulder. "You're a good influence on him, Hannah. Whatever else happens, I hope you'll remember that."

VIPER HAD NEVER been more ill-tempered, and Colin wondered if the horse was somehow picking up on *his* mood tonight. Somehow, Hannah and Justin had talked him into an evening ride to show his brother the ranch. Alone, either one of them were difficult to argue with, but both together? Besides, he hadn't put up much of a fight. Being out here was preferable to being inside. Justin's presence seemed to shrink the house. Colin had been battling a punishing sense of claustrophobia all afternoon.

In an act of petty revenge, he'd saddled Apples for his brother. Next to the elderly Mavis, Apples was the slowest horse on the ranch. On a good day, Viper could leave her in the dust. But tonight, Viper wasn't himself. There seemed to be a conspiracy to force Colin into his brother's company. Colin half listened while Justin talked about house hunting and the place he and Elisabeth found. After the wedding, he'd be moving out of his rental home and Elisabeth's twin sister was moving into the loft where Elisabeth and Kaylee currently lived.

Eventually, Justin wound down. There was an expectant pause, and Colin knew it was his turn to talk.

He didn't have anything he wanted to say. Instead, he let the silence build around him like a protective wall.

He should have known his brother wouldn't be deterred so easily.

"So." Justin cleared her throat. "She's a beautiful woman, and a damn good cook."

"I am not discussing Hannah with you."

"I suppose the fact she has a kid is also off-limits?" Justin sighed. "When I got here this afternoon, I jumped to the conclusion that Arden had been overreacting. You look good, bro, better than I've seen you in a long time. But, now? I think maybe our sister was right to worry. Giving Hannah the cold shoulder isn't fair. It's not her fault I'm here."

Maybe not, but why had she invited him to stay the night? Because she was Hannah. *She's bighearted and generous and willing to take in strays.* During a conversation about Scarlett, he'd realized she'd adopted the ugly mutt because she'd been afraid no one else would. Given her history as a foster child, it was understandable that she worked so hard to make everyone feel welcome. In fact, it was one of the qualities he lov—

It was one of the qualities he admired about her. At least, he admired it when the person she was welcoming wasn't his annoying younger brother.

"I'm not giving Hannah the cold shoulder," he said. But the guilty note in his tone was unmistakable. He wasn't angry with her. He just...

"You've looked strung out since her kid came home from the movies," Justin said. "Does she know about—"

"Yes!" In deference to the horses, Colin quickly lowered his voice. But it shook with unwanted emotion.

"Hannah knows everything. I've talked, I've shared. So get off my back."

Peace and quiet prevailed, but the lack of conversation wasn't as soothing as Colin had hoped. Justin had punctured his cocoon of denial. It was easier to compartmentalize the facets of his life around Todd and Henry, people who knew him only as a ranch hand, not as someone's husband. Meshing who he used to be with the life he had now was more difficult with Justin here to witness it.

His brother had been the best man at Colin's wedding. Now things were coming full circle in a way that left him queasy. Had he been trying to replace the wife and son he'd lost with Hannah and Evan?

"After Mom died," Colin said, "one of my first acts of taking care of you or Arden was this splinter you got in your foot. Really deep. Dad was so submerged in grief that I think we could have accidentally amputated our thumbs and he wouldn't have noticed. But the splinter caused you pain when you walked, and I was determined to help you get it out. Every time I came near it, you wailed like the biggest wimp on earth."

"I have no recollection of this. I think you're making it up."

Colin snorted. They both knew better. "It's like I've had a splinter in my heart," he said haltingly. "It got worse and worse and worse for two years, infected probably. And Hannah somehow drew it to the surface. She has this way of getting me to talk—about the accident, about random stuff like picking out nursery furniture before Danny was born. She's not only extracting the memories but the pain."

"She helped you heal." Justin said it with pride and awe.

"Maybe I'm not ready to give up the pain." Once he did, Natalie and Danny would be *gone*. "That sounded stupid. Of course, I don't want to be miserable. But before I came here, I thought I had a handle on who I was. Hannah's changing me."

"Like that's a bad thing?" Justin muttered. "I loved Natalie and Danny, too, you know. They were family. But she wouldn't have wanted pain for you. It's selfish to want it for yourself."

Colin bit back a retort, knowing his brother meant well.

"I'll leave in the morning," Justin said. "I'll tell Arden you've been holding a steady job for a month and seem to be doing well. But in the name of pointless optimism, let me remind you that you're entitled to bring a plus-one to the wedding. Actually, since you're the best man, I think you might even rate a plus-two. Kaylee would love having someone close to her own age there. Don't answer now," he added hastily when Colin started to speak. "Just think about it. I would consider it my wedding present from you if you bring Hannah to the ceremony."

"That's not a good enough reason to bring her," Colin said. He wouldn't mislead her about the depth of their relationship, not even as a favor to his brother.

Irked, Justin rode on ahead, but his voice carried when he called back, "Bro, from where I'm sitting, you don't have a worthwhile reason *not* to bring her."

HANNAH WASN'T SURPRISED when Colin turned in early for the night. With his brother sleeping in the room next to him, there had been no chance he'd invite Hannah into his bed. Still, logic didn't stop her from lying awake long past midnight, on the slim hope that he might knock on her bedroom door. His scent lingered on her sheets and the memories of what they'd done in this very bed earlier in the day tormented her.

It would be easy to blame Justin for his inconvenient timing, but with or without his showing up, the end result was going to be the same. She would lose Colin. He'd never made any secret that he wasn't the kind of guy to stick around in one place. He'd always planned to leave for his brother's wedding and that job afterward on a cattle drive. Although she'd enjoyed hearing Justin's anecdotes about wedding plans, each one reminded her that the big day was rapidly approaching.

Her time with Colin was almost at an end.

She blinked rapidly, trying to catch her tears on her lashes. It didn't count as crying over the cowboy if the tears didn't actually make it to her cheeks.

Find a bright side, her inner voice urged. Like…the ranch was in far better shape than it had been before Colin came.

But what about me? What shape would her heart be in once he'd gone? Maybe she should be proactive. Since she wasn't sleeping anyway, she would work on the wording for a new "help wanted" ad. Or edit her to-do list to reflect what she'd accomplished over the past few days and rank the improvements she wanted to tackle next, ordering her short-term goals.

To Do: Get over Colin Cade. That was priority number one. No, wait. Technically, it was number two. Step one was figuring out *how.*

By the time Hannah's alarm clock blared at her in the morning, she felt as if she'd had only twenty minutes of sleep.

Breakfast was a subdued affair. Justin kept shooting worried glances at Colin, who barely said two words, and Hannah yawned her way through every sentence she said. Even Evan seemed affected by the gloomy mood. As he had the night before, Justin helped her clear plates off the table then teased her about not letting him help load the dishwasher.

Then it was time to say goodbye to him. The thought made her unaccountably sad—probably because she knew she was unlikely to see him again. She wouldn't have a chance to meet Elisabeth or Kaylee or Arden. In bits and pieces over the past month, Colin had told her so much about his family that she felt as if she knew them. But that was only a pleasant fantasy.

Justin hugged her on the front porch. "It was wonderful to meet you. You're a special woman, Hannah Shaw."

She swallowed the lump in her throat. "If you ever find yourself in Bingham Pass again, come say hi. You're always welcome here."

He nodded. "I'll keep that in mind. I don't have any immediate plans to return, but that's the funny thing about life. You just never know, do you?"

Biting her lip, she refrained from answering. It was true that life had thrown plenty of curveballs at her, some devastating, others wonderful. And some, like Colin, were both.

Plenty of people claimed that gardening was therapeutic, and, after Justin had driven away, Hannah tried to immerse herself in caring for the plants and vegetables. She tried not to feel miffed that she barely saw Colin all day, battling back an unwelcome wave of neediness. *He's* supposed *to be tending to the cattle and horses, remember? That's his job.*

When evening rolled around, however, and he was still making himself scarce, she was forced to admit he was deliberately avoiding her. She and Evan were halfway through dinner when Colin entered the house. He didn't stay long enough even to eat with them, only to grab his pillow and a few other supplies.

"I'm worried about Viper," he told her. "He was rolling earlier and wasn't himself last night. It may be colic. I'm going to sleep down at the stable to keep a better eye on him."

She wanted to scream. Was sleeping on the rockhard, hay-strewn ground really preferable to sharing the same house with her? She wasn't planning on attacking him, for pity's sake. Hannah had her pride.

She met his gaze, not bothering to hide her frustration. "Do what you have to do."

He faltered, looking as if he might say more, but ultimately, he shook his head and walked away. Just as she'd known he would.

Sirens.

The jarring Klaxon cry penetrated Colin's sleep, along with the sound of nervous whinnies. And…the smell of smoke?

Colin sat bolt upright. Tonight was like an encore of the months of nightmares he'd experienced, except this time, instead of waking from one, he was waking *to* it. Smoke and sirens meant a fire.

He ran from the stable and saw fire trucks rolling up in front of the main house—which was ablaze. *Jesus, no.* Hannah and Evan! Heart and legs pumping in wild tandem, he sprinted for the house. *No, no, no, not again.* He hadn't been there to get them out safely. He'd failed them. Terror was like ice in his veins.

When he got close enough to see a tear-stained Hannah talking to a fireman, Evan at her side clasping Trainket in his small hands, the stark relief nearly drove Colin to his knees. They were alive. They were okay. But the adrenaline and fear lingered like a nauseating aftertaste.

When he got closer, Hannah saw him. Despite how aloof he'd been with her for the past two days—*face it, you've been an ass*—she rushed toward him and threw her arms around him. That was Hannah. She met life head-on, with faith and forgiveness. She was far too good for him.

He stroked a shaking hand over her hair, furious that she smelled like smoke instead of vanilla. "Are you okay?" Some of his anger that she couldn't catch a break seeped into his gruff tone.

"We're all right." The brave words contrasted with the tremor in her voice, the clamminess of her skin. "I got Evan and Scarlett out safely, and the firemen are containing the blaze to the left side of the house."

The fire wasn't out yet, but it was already noticeably weaker than when he'd caught his first heart-stopping glimpse of it. Still, it had been a dry year. Colin wouldn't breathe easy again until every last spark had been dampened.

"It started upstairs," she said. "I'm glad you weren't there."

Her soft words triggered a spike of guilt. If he *had* slept in his usual bed, maybe he would have noticed it faster, helped put it out before it engulfed the guest rooms she'd been so diligently renovating.

"Th-they think m-maybe a short in the wiring." Her teeth were chattering, and he pulled her closer. "Until recently, I hadn't been in those rooms much, so I wasn't using the electricity up there. On the br-bright side…" She gulped, and he realized that she was about to lose it completely.

"Hannah, it's okay. You can be strong tomorrow. For now—"

"On the bright side," she continued with almost hysterical determination, "we may not lose many of our personal belongings." Her and Evan's rooms were at the opposite end of the house. "But it looks like those guest rooms won't be open for new business anytime soon, huh?" Then she laughed. Which quickly became a sob.

"Colin?" Evan's voice was scared. "Is Mommy okay?"

That cut through Hannah's mini breakdown better than anything Colin could have said—not that he was full of wise words at the moment. Mostly he wanted to shake his fist at the sky and scream obscenities. He was so damn sick of bad things happening to good people. And even though his fear should have ebbed once he saw that Hannah and Evan were all right, it was still there. In fact, it was crippling, ballooning ever larger. How had he put himself in a position to lose someone else? Anguish over the past, coupled with the tragedy that could have happened here tonight, knifed through him.

Hadn't he learned his lesson by now? He'd told his brother he wasn't sure if he were truly ready to let go of the pain. But he'd been lying to himself. The truth was, he wasn't ready to risk that pain again. Not now, not ever.

"I'm okay," Hannah was assuring her son. "But we're going to have a sleepover at Aunt Annette's tonight once we're done here. Colin, will you drive us? I'm...a little shaky."

She made the admission with a twinge of embarrassment that blew his mind. Her house had almost burned down around her! Of course, she was shaky.

"I'll get you there safely," he promised.

Driving her across town was the perfect task for him—a concrete, unemotional form of assistance. That, he could handle. But he suspected it was one of the last things he'd be able to do for Hannah Shaw. She had too many other needs that required dangerous involvement outside his skill set.

Life was precarious. And his was better lived alone.

SEEING THE FIRE damage in the harsh light of day made Colin's stomach buckle. Annette was bringing Evan by shortly so that he could see his home was still there, but Hannah had wanted to inspect the aftermath of the fire herself first. Colin almost gagged at the lingering stench of smoke. It would be a long, long time before he ate barbecue or roasted marshmallows again.

Hannah sat at the bottom of the staircase, wringing her hands. Behind her, the wall panel he'd built to give her better pipe access was now a charred black patch. "I am so sorry." It hadn't occurred to them until they'd reached Annette's house that *he'd* lost belongings in the blaze.

"Don't worry about me. I didn't have that much," he reminded her. Many of his belongings were in storage.

He'd learned the importance of traveling light. It was a lesson he didn't intend to forget again. "Still got my hat. And my motorcycle helmet."

She flinched at the reference to his motorcycle. Because they both knew he'd be riding away soon?

"You lost your sketch pad, though."

He forced a shrug. "They were just doodles when you come right down to it."

"That's *not* all they were! That picture you did for my birthday? It inspired me, gave me hope. But now... God. Maybe it's time for me to face facts. We've already had our own versions of flood and fire. Instead of locusts, I have the killer bull."

Seeing her so defeated caused an ache inside him. He knelt in front of her, trying to coax a smile. "We've arranged a buyer for Beelzebull, remember? The rest can be dealt with, too. Your conversation with the insurance company seemed to go really well this morning. Don't give up."

"Why not?" She leveled him with her damp hazel eyes. "You are."

He backed away, stricken. "Don't put that on me. You *knew* I was going." He raked a hand through his hair. "I helped with the bull, got the cows wormed over the weekend. Viper's doing better, and I put in a call to my buddy Dwayne to see if he wants some temporary work helping you out. He's a seasoned hand, like Henry, but only in his early forties. He may be a good fit."

"*You* were a good fit," she persisted, rising to her feet. "Not just on this ranch, but in my life. Colin, I—"

"Please don't." He shook his head wildly.

She took a deep breath, clenching and relaxing her fists at her sides, but her tone was no calmer when she spoke. "I know you have the wedding, and I know you're scheduled to help with the drive. But give me one good reason why you couldn't come back after that. Assuming an asteroid hasn't taken out the house by then."

It was the most bitter she'd ever sounded, and he wondered whether the fire was behind the broken note in her voice or if it was his fault. He knew of *two* good reasons he couldn't be here: her and Evan. They were both stealing his heart, and he couldn't protect it from further damage if he allowed that to happen.

"Don't you feel anything for me?" she pressed.

It was the worst thing she could have said.

"Of course I do! But I don't *want* to, Hannah. If you or Evan had been… You could have…" He couldn't voice the words. His brain skittered away from even thinking them. Since last night, some part of him had been curled into a ball, rocking back and forth in a dark corner of his mind, trying to numb itself instead of allowing him to think about the possibilities. He didn't have to impress Hannah; he merely had to cope.

She took his hand. "The worst didn't happen. I don't have so much as a twisted ankle this time. We're *okay.*"

I'm not. For the past week, living on optimism he'd borrowed from her, he'd thought maybe he could be. But it was time to return the rose-colored glasses to their rightful owner. Colin had lost both his parents, his wife and his son. He would not voluntarily put himself in a position to lose anyone else.

No matter how much he loved her.

HANNAH HAD BEEN through a lot since the day she and Evan had moved onto the ranch. Plumbing disasters, the guilt of Henry being injured by an animal she owned, a damn *fire* for cripes' sake. But none of it had been as difficult to endure as watching Colin Cade drive away on a sunny Wednesday afternoon.

She'd actually envied Evan his freedom to cry when he'd hugged Colin one final time. Her son had sniffled and whined about the unfairness of it. Hannah, on the other hand, had resigned herself to doing the mature thing—wishing Colin well and thanking him for his help.

"You may not have been here long," she'd said, "but the impact you've made is immeasurable." She wished she could have read his expression better, but it was difficult to see his eyes through his dark sunglasses. Colin was a master at finding ways to shut people out—from not answering phone calls to jumping on his motorcycle and fleeing when a situation became too intimate for him to handle.

Even his kiss goodbye had been detached, a quick brush of his lips over her forehead, nowhere in the vicinity of her mouth, as if he was deliberately avoiding any memory of the passion they'd shared.

"Hey? You doing okay?" Annette stepped onto the porch, giving Hannah a half hug. "I've got Evan settled with some cartoons and chocolate doughnuts, so we have a few minutes for venting. If you'd like to call your former ranch hand some obscene names, I have suggestions."

That offer drew a watery chuckle from Hannah. But she ended up defending him. "Colin's not a bad guy. He's just been through a hell of a lot."

"Yes, but now he's putting you through a lot. As your best friend, I'm entitled to be annoyed with him. You guys were *good* together."

We really were. "I think he knows that. I even think it's part of the problem. He doesn't want a relationship, doesn't want to be vulnerable to anyone."

"Then he's going to be a very lonely man."

Hannah met her friend's eyes. "He already is. I thought I could fix that, but I was being arrogant."

She was a single mom and a struggling ranch owner with ambition and baking skill. She was not a miracle worker.

Chapter Fourteen

Justin's automatic smile of greeting crumpled when he stepped outside and got a better look at Colin's face beneath the porch light. "Oh, hell. You blew it with Hannah, didn't you?"

"Coming here was a mistake," Colin growled. "Cielo Peak's got plenty of hotels."

His brother reached out and grabbed his elbow. "Get inside and tell me all about it, you idiot."

Colin had spent the entire ride to Cielo Peak calling himself far worse names. When he relived Hannah's wounded expression as she told him goodbye, he hated himself for ever kissing her, much less making love to her. He was a selfish SOB. By indulging his own desires, he'd hurt her in the process.

He'd rationalized that as long as he was honest with her about his intentions, he couldn't break her heart, but he'd known better. He'd known from the beginning that Hannah was open and loving and full of hope. If he'd destroyed that hope, like some blindly rampaging beast trampling a beautiful flower garden—

"Yo!" Justin snapped his fingers in front of his face. "You haven't answered anything I've said for the last two minutes. Have you gone catatonic on me?"

"No." But that might be an improvement.

"Well, then get inside," Justin repeated. "We can do this the easy way, which involves you and me sitting at my kitchen table over a couple of beers, or the hard way."

"Which would be…?"

His brother gave him a menacing grin. "Me calling Arden and telling her she's needed for an emotional intervention."

"You are a heartless bastard." Nonetheless, Colin followed him inside.

"Before Elisabeth, I think that was true. I was charming when I wanted to be, but mostly heartless. Beth's made me a better man. I saw glimmers of hope that Hannah was restoring *you* to a better version of yourself." He popped the lids off of two bottles of beer with a magnetized opener he kept on the fridge, then slid a bottle across the table to Colin. "Why are you here instead of with her?"

"I was coming for the wedding anyway."

"Not until next week. Cut the crap, and tell me the truth."

"Her house caught fire." Even after seeing it with his own eyes, the words were surreal.

Justin's eyes widened in alarm. "Is she okay? Is Evan—"

"They're all right." Thank God. "But what you're feeling right now? Magnify that by a million, and you'll start to get an inkling of how I felt." Colin knocked back a quarter of his beer, but it was nowhere near strong enough to dull the edge of panic that had taken up residence inside his chest. It was as if he were trying to breathe around a lungful of razor blades. "Justin, I can't go through that again."

His brother sat back in his chair, looking troubled. "I hear what you're saying, and I understand it. But it's a load of manure. What's your plan, to not give a damn about anyone else for the next fifty or sixty years? What about me and Arden? Or have you already decided you don't care about us? That would explain moving away and never answering your freaking phone."

Colin recoiled. "You know how important the two of you are to me!"

"And if I break my neck skiing, would it make you sorry we were brothers? Would you undo that bond now if you could, to prevent having to mourn me later?"

"After everyone we've buried, how dare you be glib about the idea of something happening to you?"

Remorse flickered across Justin's face, but he didn't back down, merely switched tactics. "Okay, forget that line of argument. Let's see how well you do debating your own words. Or don't you remember that verbal ass-kicking you gave me when I almost let Beth slip away?"

Colin downed more of his beer, telling himself the two situations were different.

"You pointed out that when you lost Natalie, you had no choice in the matter, no opportunity to fight for her, whereas I was just too chicken to fight for Elisabeth. *You* could be fighting for Hannah now! You could be building a life with her. I saw the way she looked at you, and that woman is in love."

Colin's throat clenched. He was torn between pure, ecstatic joy and sheer horror that Hannah could love him. "She deserves better."

"Then *be* better. You told me at Christmas that you

would have traded anything for one more day, one more hour with Natalie. I'm not saying Hannah's a substitute for her—Natalie and Danny are irreplaceable—but life has given you a second chance! There is a wonderful woman out there with the incredibly bad taste to adore you, and you're letting the hours and days you could have with her slip away."

Although Justin was making a lot of sense, it was difficult for reason to combat panic. "It's not as easy as you're making it sound."

"Of course not." Justin's smile was sympathetic. "Love takes work, and when it's real love, it's damn scary."

Then Colin's feelings for Hannah Shaw must be very, very real. But how could he find the courage to do anything about them?

COLIN HAD BARELY slept a wink when his brother got up the next morning for work. They exchanged nods while the smell of brewing coffee filled the kitchen, but neither attempted actual conversation until they had caffeine running through their veins.

Once Justin drained his mug, he seemed sufficiently awake to start worrying. "I hate to leave you here by yourself all day."

Colin rolled his eyes. "I'm a grown man, not an unsupervised toddler."

"I know. But if you need me to take the afternoon off or—"

"Quit. The best man isn't supposed to be a burden on the groom-to-be. It's the other way around. Don't you have something useful I can do?"

"Now that you mention it..." Justin glanced around

the kitchen. A large cardboard box, marked KITCHEN, was sealed and sitting against one wall. Another box, sitting open, took up a big chunk of counter space. "The Donnellys and a couple of guys from my patrol are coming the day after tomorrow to help move stuff, and I'm not finished packing yet. I ran out of tape and paper to wrap the dishes and glass stuff. You can take that over if you need a distraction."

It was clear from Justin's knowing tone that he meant a distraction from thinking about Hannah. Which Colin was *not* going to do. Except for the thought he'd just had...and the roughly two thousand other thoughts that had plagued him during the night.

Her expression as she'd said goodbye haunted him. He wanted to pick up the phone and make sure she was all right. A clean break seemed less selfish, though.

"Packing," he said. "I'm on it."

Once Justin left, Colin made a quick run to town for supplies, eager to have something to do.

When he returned, wrapping plates and stacking them inside the box gave him a soothing sense of purpose. But it didn't take long for the silence of the house to press in around him. He'd become accustomed to Evan's chatter and the background noise of Hannah's mixer whirring or the metallic slide of a cookie sheet going into the oven. Even when Colin had been busy outdoors, there'd been the nickering of horses or—

A frustrated snarl escaped him. Why couldn't he go five minutes without thinking of Hannah and her ranch? *Give it time.* After all, he'd said goodbye to her only yesterday.

He loaded the packing tape into the sharp-edged dispenser so that he could seal up the box. The abrasive sound of tape being stretched across the seam of cardboard and then ripped away from the roll was distinctive. It filled him with a sense of déjà vu. Not too long ago, he and Justin had helped Arden pack up her belongings as she prepared to move to Garrett's ranch.

You packed up your own boxes, too. Colin had a lot of stuff in storage. It seemed an apt metaphor for his life. His siblings were moving on, moving forward to be with the people they loved. Colin was in stasis, his untouched possessions growing musty in a dark, padlocked unit he never visited.

He used to hear Natalie's voice in his head on a fairly regular basis, imagining what she might say to him, but it had been weeks. Now, in the unnatural stillness of Justin's house, he could hear her exasperated tone loud and clear. *The worst part isn't that our stuff is neglected and forgotten—it's just stuff. No, the worst part is that* you're *moldering away. Life is short. And you're squandering it.*

Colin knew better than most how fleeting life could be, yet he was here while so many others had died too young. He glared at the tape roller in his hand. If he didn't start building a real life instead of drifting from place to place, he might as well box up his heart and shove it in that storage unit alongside the furniture and old photo albums. He owed it to the people he'd lost— owed it to *himself*—to live and be happy. And to love.

THE INSURANCE SETTLEMENT was going to be more generous than Hannah had expected. She tried to use that discovery to buoy her battered optimism as she strolled into the town diner at noon on Saturday. She had a lunch appointment to interview the man Colin had recom-

mended. Dwayne had sounded competent and genu-
inely interested over the phone. Maybe it would go well,
and this man would be a solid replacement for Henry.

Positive thoughts, Hannah!

Ever since Colin had abandoned them, she'd been
trying to remain upbeat and cheerful. Evan was in a
fragile place right now, with his idol gone and the second story of their house a charred mess. But even as
she smiled brightly and kept her tone chipper, Hannah
fantasized about crawling into a pair of ratty sweats
and hiding under her comforter with a gallon or three
of ice cream.

Unfortunately, she doubted that Ben and Jerry, wonderful though they may be, were going to help repair
her roof, clean her walls or replace her furniture. So it
was up to her to keep moving forward. Stubborn anger
helped. She was not going to give up at the first sign of
trouble like Colin Cade, the man who—*was sitting at
a booth in the Bingham Pass diner?*

Hannah's pulse went into overdrive. For a moment,
she was afraid she might hyperventilate. When she
froze in her tracks, Colin rose and came to her. Her
feet hadn't figured out how to move yet, but her eyes
roved over him, avidly taking in every detail. He looked
so good, and she'd missed him so much. The four days
since she'd seen him felt like a lifetime.

"I—I was supposed to be meeting Dwayne," she
stammered. This couldn't be a coincidence, Colin just
happening to be at the diner when she walked in.

"About that." He tipped his straw hat back on his
head. "He and I were talking, and I suggested to him
that you may not have a position available after all."

"You did what?" Annoyance spurted at his heavy-handedness. He'd refused to consider staying on long-term, but he was running off the first man who'd seriously considered it?

"It's all right, though. I got him a paying gig on a cattle drive."

A cattle drive? Such as the one he was scheduled to leave for right after Justin's wedding? "So...the two of you will be working together?" she asked cautiously.

"Nope."

Feeling a little weak in the knees, she slid into the booth. Colin sat across from her, his expression unreadable. It wasn't cold or aloof, though—quite the opposite. So many emotions danced in his blue-green eyes that she couldn't catalogue them all.

She hoped the waitress brought them glasses of water soon. Her mouth had gone bone-dry. "Colin, what are you doing here?"

"Applying for a job."

Her heart wrenched. A month ago, that would have been the answer to her prayers. After everything they'd shared, however, she didn't think she could hire him. Any possibility of a platonic, professional relationship had been shot to hell. "I'm not sure that's a good idea."

He nodded solemnly. "I understand why you would feel that way. But since I'm here, would you humor me by taking a peek at my résumé? I'd appreciate the feedback." He opened a folder she hadn't noticed until then and handed her a crisp sheet of paper.

She stared at it uncomprehendingly, not really seeing the words but needing the chance to recover her composure. But when her eyes landed on a section halfway down the page that read "Related skills: Thorough lover," her cheeks flamed and any chance of poise disappeared. "Is this some kind of joke?" She lowered her voice to an angry hiss. "I was paying you for the work you did on the ranch, not the…you know, other stuff."

"No joke. Did you start at the top with my mission statement?"

Her gaze flew to the words she'd overlooked, and her heart melted. In the boldfaced statement, he'd proclaimed his objective of "fearlessly loving Hannah Shaw" and earning her love in return, standing beside her and braving whatever life threw their way.

"Oh, Colin." Taking her time, she read over the page, each of the heartfelt bullet points heightening the profound joy unfurling inside her. "You could've just picked up the phone and said all of this to me."

"I'm not sure I could have," he admitted. "I needed time to think it through, to try to put my feelings into words and actions. It's been an enlightening week."

"Really?" she asked drily. "My week's been pure hell."

He reached for her hand atop the table, his thumb stroking over the pulse point at her wrist. "I'm sorry I put you through that. I know you don't have any proof, so these may be empty words, but for what it's worth, I think I was getting there—to a place where I could love you freely, where I could let myself be loved. But then Justin showing up, the fire happening… I panicked."

"I do believe you." She'd always had more faith in him than he'd had in himself. And she'd witnessed firsthand how his smiles had come more easily each day, his growing affection with not only her but others around him. He'd made a place for himself where he belonged—only he hadn't wanted it. "What changed your mind?"

"Other than seeing your face in my head every waking hour, not being able to sleep without dreaming of you and my brother consistently reminding me that I was an idiot for leaving?" He shrugged. "Boxes."

She cocked her head, waiting for him to elaborate.

"Justin's moving. Both my siblings are moving forward, and I've been standing still. Maybe that didn't matter to me before because I didn't have anyplace I wanted to be, anyone I wanted to be *with*—but now there's you. Hannah, I'm sorry. And I don't want to waste one more day being without you."

Tears misting her vision, she bounced out of her seat and rushed to his side of the booth to hug him. "I missed you so much," she whispered.

He captured her mouth in a kiss that told her the feeling was mutual. His tongue delved between her lips, and the kiss became more urgent. Need spiraled through her. She longed for a physical closeness that matched the candid intimacy of his words. When he nipped at her earlobe, she groaned in frustration.

"I love you," she said. "Please don't take this the wrong way, but *why* did you have to pick a public diner for this reunion?"

He pulled back with a grin. "No one's come to take our order yet. Would it be an inappropriate time to mention that my child-free hotel room is within walking distance?"

She grabbed his hand. "Then what are we still doing here?"

Fingers laced together, they hurried from the diner and into the sunshine, into their future.

Epilogue

The wedding was beautiful, but Hannah felt a little guilty for her wandering attention. Instead of focusing on the bride and groom, her gaze continually strayed to the gorgeous best man. In her opinion, Colin Cade was the sexiest man in all of Colorado. He was gorgeous in his tux, but she was looking forward to the next time she saw him in jeans and that cowboy hat, too.

When the ceremony ended, guests began heading to the reception at the Donnelly Ski Lodge. The wedding party stayed behind for pictures, and Evan and Kaylee—who'd taken to each other instantly—asked for permission to play tag just outside the chapel. Hannah sat in one of the pews, keeping one eye on the kids through the window while listening to the photographer cajole smiles and chuckles from the bridal party.

Arden Cade Frost was every bit as lovely and spirited as Hannah had imagined. The two women had been seated next to each other at Justin and Elisabeth's rehearsal dinner. Colin had groaned at the arrangements, seemingly worried that if Hannah and his sister ever ganged up on him, he was doomed. Today, poor Arden had sobbed through the entire ceremony. As she'd pointed out beforehand, now that she was pregnant, she found herself weeping over just about everything. She loudly instructed the photographer to fix her red nose and watery eyes with digital editing.

When all the pictures were done, members of the wedding party and their escorts headed for the appropriate vehicles. Colin had surprised Hannah on the drive to Cielo Peak by suggesting that if they sold her truck and his motorcycle, they might have enough money for a substantial vehicular upgrade.

"You'd sell your motorcycle?" she'd asked.

His reply had been a cryptic, "I don't need it anymore."

Elisabeth's adopted daughter, Kaylee, was supposed to ride with the bride and groom but, at the last second, asked if she could go "in Evan's car." The newlyweds seemed happy about the prospect of a few minutes alone, provided Colin and Hannah didn't mind.

"It's fine with us," Hannah assured them. Although neither brother had revealed the specifics of the conversation, she knew Justin had said some things to Colin that had really resonated, helping to bring him back to Hannah. She would always be grateful to Justin for that.

During the brief car ride, Kaylee and Evan discussed bowling.

"Maybe you can come with us next time," Evan told his new friend.

"I've never been before," Kaylee said, "but I'm sure I'd be very good at it."

Behind the wheel of the car, Colin laughed. "Looks like someone else is a student of positive thinking."

As he parked in front of the lodge, Hannah's cell phone chimed. She pulled it out of her purse and discovered that Annette had texted her a photo. It took Hannah a moment to identify what she was looking at—a tapered, white stick with two red lines showing in a circle. It was captioned TWO LINES!!!!!!

A smile split her face. "Guess who's going to be an honorary aunt?" she whispered to Colin.

He grinned back at her, and she took a mental snapshot, wanting to hold on to this moment. It had been a beautiful day. She was surrounded by wonderful people, including her son and the man she loved. Her best friend was going to have a baby. She was brimming with happiness.

Thirty minutes later, Colin stirred even more emotion within her when he lifted his glass of champagne and gave his toast as best man.

"As many of you know already, for a long time, Justin, Arden and I only had each other. Some days it felt like the three of us against the world. I believed family was the most important thing in life. I still do—but that family has expanded. Our circle of three has grown to include some magnificent people, like the beautiful Elisabeth Donnelly Cade."

The bride beamed at him.

"There was a time, not that long ago, when I would have wondered if a step like marriage was too drastic. Loving someone else so completely opens up the risk of being hurt." Colin's blue-green eyes sought out Hannah in the crowd. "What I'd forgotten is that loving someone else is also the only way to reap life's most incredible rewards. Justin and Elisabeth, you are an inspiration. Thank you for reminding us all that happily-ever-afters aren't fairy tales. They're real for anyone brave enough to work for them. My suggestion to you for many blissful years together is to treat each other with respect, live each day with a sense of humor and always remember to look on the bright side."

* * * * *